Good God. Vickie just called. The galleys for the first quarter of the book, exclusive of artwork, will arrive at Craig from the typesetter in Pennsylvania some time tomorrow afternoon. Vickie has volunteered—there was simply no way I could say no—to bring them out to Fire Island on Saturday.

I am to go over the galleys, according to this plan, while Vickie sunbathes the weekend away. On the afternoon of Monday, the Fourth of July, she will carry the corrected galleys back to New York; mission accomplished. I did explain that we were already pretty crowded out there, but she said that was okay, she didn't mind, she'd bring a sleeping bag and just bunk on the living room floor.

This is insane. Where do you go to enlist in the Foreign Legion? I am going to be in that small rented house over the Fourth of July weekend with Mary *and* Ginger *and* VICKIE! What kind of Independence Day do you call *that*?

A LIKELY STORY

Look for all these Tor books by Donald E. Westlake

KAHAWA
WHY ME
LEVINE
A LIKELY STORY
HIGH ADVENTURE

DONALD E. WESTLAKE

A LIKELY STORY

TOR

A TOM DOHERTY ASSOCIATES BOOK

A LIKELY STORY

Copyright © 1984 by Donald E. Westlake

Reprinted by arrangement with Penzler Books

First Tor printing: November 1986

A TOR Book

Published by Tom Doherty Associates, Inc.
49 West 24 Street
New York, N.Y. 10010

ISBN: 0-812-51058-5
CAN. ED.: 0-812-51059-3

Library of Congress Catalog Card Number: 84-61250

Printed in the United States

0 9 8 7 6 5 4 3 2 1

This is for
   Justin Scott
   Joe Gores
   Brian Garfield
   Hal Dresner
   Al Collins
   and
   Larry Block
and for two superb editors
   Lee Wright
   and
   Rich Barber

I'll publish, right or wrong:
Fools are my theme, let satire be my song.
—*Lord Byron*

The fickleness of the women I love is only
equalled by the infernal constancy of the
women who love me.
—*George Bernard Shaw*

Notice to the Reader, and His Attorney

THIS is a work of fiction. All of the characters in this book are fictional, and my creation. Some of these characters wear the names of famous real persons. I have not attempted to describe the true personal characteristics of these famous real persons, whom in most instances I do not know. In each case, I have put that famous name with what I take to be the *public perception* of that individual. (The equivalent, for instance, of suggesting that Jack Benny the person was really a tightwad, though in fact his public persona was that of a tightwad while he was very generous in private life.)

I have deliberately chosen not to follow the accepted pattern of changing the name and keeping the public personality, to have a baseball pitcher named Jim Beaver, for instance, who led the Mets to the World Series in 1969. I think that method is arch, crass and deplorable.

The famous names herein are just that: famous names. In looking behind them, the reader will not find the actual human beings who hold those names, nor satires on those human beings. The reader will find only what I believe is the generally held view of that famous name's public self.

The same, of course, is true of the obscure characters within this book. As for myself, gentle reader, I am a figment of *your* imagination.

Books by Tom Diskant

The Pink Garage Gang (novel)
Coral Sea
El Alamein
Golf Courses of America
The Ins and Outs of Unemployment Insurance
Rumble Seats and Running Boards: The Wheels
   of Yesteryear
Hospitals Can Make You Sick
The Films of Jack Oakie
The Christmas Book

~~~~~~~~~~~~~~~

Tuesday, January 4th

"NEVER write a novel in the first person," Jack told me.

"I know that," I said. "And never write a novel in diary form either."

"An you shoah got to keep out ub dialect."

Oh, how we amused ourselves. Just a couple of old pals having lunch together, that's all, good old roly-poly Jack Rosenfarb and the present speaker, Tom Diskant, chuckling over our sole *Veronique* and house chablis and letting the old real world just go hang. A comedy team at leisure, one skinny and the other stout, I Jack Spratt to his missus, Stan to his Ollie, André to his Wallace Shawn.

The reality, of course, was quite different. Good old Jack was an editor with the publishing firm of Craig, Harry & Bourke, the firm was picking up the check, and I was there,

13

heart and sole in my mouth, to peddle a book.

"Well, the novel's dead anyway," I said. "I wouldn't come here to talk to you about a novel."

"Bless you, Tom," he said, his merry eyes crinkling. "You always know what to say."

I hesitated. We both waited for me to tell him what book I wanted him to buy. This was the moment of truth—well, in a manner of speaking—and I hated and feared the upcoming instant of either acceptance or rejection. What if he said no? Time was pleasant now, in the predecision phase, wining and dining and making jokes. Outside, the world was black and white and wet with January slush under a sky piled with round gray clouds like full laundry bags, cars and buildings all were speckled with city mud on a Park Avenue so dark and desolate and grim one automatically looked for tumbrels, but here inside the Tre Mafiosi all was warm and good, gold and ivory and pale, pale green.

Oh, well; man does not live by lunch alone. "It's a Christmas book," I mumbled, and chugged chablis.

Jack's merry twinkle faded. He looked puzzled, faintly troubled, as though afraid he was about to hear—or have to give—some bad news. "It's a what?" he asked.

"Christmas," I said. "A Christmas book."

"Oh, Lord," he said, laughing, but hollowly. "Haven't we had enough of all that? We're

getting the damn tree out tomorrow, at long
last. Twelfth Night. The fucking thing is *naked*,
Tom, there's green needles everywhere I turn,
they're in the fucking *bed*."

"Christmas will return," I said.

"Say not so."

"But it will, Jack. Along about May, the folks
at Craig are all going to start saying, 'What've
we got for Christmas? We need a Christmas
book. A big glossy picture-full star-studded
Christmas-gift coffee-table book, twenty-nine
fifty until January first.'"

"Thirty-four fifty."

"Whatever." Talking, starting, under way, I
was beginning to get my confidence back.
"Look, Jack," I said. "We have had Marc
Chagall's stained glass people flying upside
down, we have had Dickens, we have had
cats, we have had feminism through the ages,
we have had gnomes, we have had cities pho-
tographed from the air, we have—"

"Please," he said. "Not a history of American publishing, not while I'm eating."

"I have the ultimate Christmas book," I said
modestly.

He thought. I watched him think, I watched
him realize that yes, May would come, and
with it the need to define the fall list, including one or more hot, pot-boiling Christmas
books. Whether or not Christmas itself would
ever return, or ever be asked back after its
most recent behavior, *May* would certainly
arrive, the need for a *fall list* was as inevitable

as death and Garfield, and he who managed to think about tomorrow today would anon be a senior editor. "The ultimate Christmas book," he murmured.

"Exactly."

He shook himself, like a dog coming out of water or an elephant waking up. "It's too late for marijuana," he said, "and the world will never be hip enough for the *Big Picture Book of Cocaine*. Orphans will continue to be out until both Vietnam and *Annie* have receded a bit further into the mists of time. The big faggot book about the apostles all being gay would probably go well at the moment, but you're the wrong guy to do it. So what's your subject?"

"Christmas," I said.

Tick. Tock. Tick. He blinked, very slowly. "You mean," he said, "a coffee table book about Christmas. A Christmas book about Christmas."

"Yes," I said simply.

"Is this a wonderful idea," he asked himself, "or is this a stupid idea?" Frowning at me, all attention, he said, "Show me this book."

I pantomimed opening the huge book. "On this page," I said, "we have a fourteenth century Madonna and Child. On the next page we have a Christmas story by Judith Krantz, especially commissioned. On the next page we have a nineteen-twenties comic prohibition Christmas card. On the next page we have an original reminiscence by Gore Vidal, Christmas in Italy, bedding the acolytes. On the next—"

"All right," he said. "I see the book. You can get these people?"

"Not without Craig, Harry & Bourke letter-head," I said.

"And money." Jack waggled a playful finger at me, as though accusing me of being naughty. "You're talking a very big advance here, buster."

"I know it, Jack."

"Excuse my saying this, Tom," Jack said, his fingers walking gingerly among the silver-ware, to show he was pussyfooting, "but that isn't your track record. The kind of advance you're talking about here, you've never had anything like this before."

Of course not. I am a journeyman writer; I will do a piece on repairing your own sink for *Ms.* magazine, sexuality among female minis-ters for *Cosmopolitan*, the rapaciousness of foot-ball team owners for *Esquire*. I did the books *Coral Sea* and *El Alamein* for the "We Go To War!" subscription series. I did *Golf Courses of America*, subsidized by American Airlines and published by Craig, Harry & Bourke, which is how I met Jack in the first place, for whom I've also done *The Ins and Outs of Unemploy-ment Insurance* and *Hospitals Can Make You Sick*.

Track record, that's all these guys talk about. It's one of their many ways to avoid original thought; if they can see what you've done before, they know what to think about you now. I had to get Jack past that bump in the road, and the only lever I could find was humility. "Sometimes, Jack," I said, "a small guy can have a big idea."

That shocked him into consciousness. "Tom, Tom," he protested, "I never said anything like *that*. This isn't you and me, this is the *company*. I'm thinking of the people I have to answer to, back in the office."

"Don't sell them *me*," I suggested. "Sell them the idea."

"There's also execution of the idea," he reminded me. "Tom, *I* know you can do whatever you set your mind to, but we've got Wilson to consider. Bourke himself. I'll level with you, Tom," he said, leaning close, looking at me with great sincerity. "If you were sitting there with a cute little idea, ten grand advance, maybe even twelve-and-a-half, one quarter on signature, we could do it in a flash. Within reason, I can close deals myself up to twenty-five grand, except even then they sometimes pull the rug out from under me. But *this*. You're talking Judith Krantz, Gore Vidal, you're talking *money*. And you need some for yourself, for God's sake, you're not doing this for charity."

"Half," I said.

He looked exceedingly blank. "What's that?"

"I figured that's the simplest way to handle it," I said. "We treat it like a regular anthology. Half the advance goes to me, the other half goes to the contributors and the research assistants and so on."

"Oh, come on, Tom," he said. "For this page, we pay Gore Vidal and we pay you the same amount? Not on."

"That's not what you're paying for," I said. "You pay Gore Vidal for that page. Me you pay for that page and for the page with the fourteenth-century Madonna and Child and for having thought it up in the first place and for talking Vidal into doing it."

"All right, possibly," he said. "If we decide to go forward at all. If the *company* decides. Then we work out the details."

"With my agent. I never talk details."

"Still Annie?"

"Yes."

"Well, she's reasonable," he said.

"I'm sorry to hear that."

"I tell you what, Tom," he said. "This is a very interesting idea, I won't deny it. Let me take it back to the shop, talk to a couple of people, do you have a presentation on paper?"

"I can't describe the contents before I send out my query letter," I pointed out. "I could do you a two-sentence memo."

"Well, we'll see."

"Jack. Jack, I came to you with this first. I did it for two reasons. I think you and Craig are absolutely right for it," I lied, "and you're almost the only person in New York I'd trust not to take the idea and run," I lied again.

"Well, we'll see." Behind his jolly eyes, his

brain was turning over like a submarine's engines.

"And if I can start *now*," I said, "we're talking about *this Christmas.*"

"Tight. Tight schedule."

"I know that. I'm up to it, Jack." I smiled at him. "What the mind of man can conceive, *this* man can do."

"I'll talk it up around the shop," he said. "And give you a call in a few days."

And that was the end of the conversation. He didn't seem wildly enthusiastic, but on the other hand he didn't reject the idea outright. And at least I've let him know I'm thinking in terms of a tight deadline. I'll give him till Monday. Or maybe Tuesday. But that's the latest.

I came home from lunch too keyed up to sit still. Ginger was at work, the kids weren't home from school yet, and I couldn't think about any of the projects currently on my desk. There was nothing in my mind but *The Christmas Book.* Oh, if Jack would only come through!

I phoned Annie, my agent, and got her answering machine. "This is the literary agency of Annie Lecadeaux," said the luxurious voice of Roger Brech-Lees, an English client, a writer of historical romances under various female names, and—*I* think—a closet queen. "Please leave your name and a phone number, and we'll get back to you as soon as we can." *Beep.*

Knowing how Annie hates hang-ups—unsatisfied curiosity eats at her vitals like the fox under the Spartan lad's tunic—I hung up without leaving a message, to punish her. Finally, I came in here to the office and started to type out the story so far. Just recounting what's going on.

I really need the money.

Wednesday, January 5th

TWELFTH Night. It's another of those ancient counting things from before they got good at math, like Easter Sunday being the third day after Good Friday. Twelfth Night is the twelfth night after Christmas, but only if you count Christmas Eve as night number one.

Anyway, Twelfth Night is the eve of the Epiphany, which celebrates two major religious moments, being the baptism of Christ and the arrival of the Three Wise Men. (It's also the date of the wedding feast at Cana, whatever that might mean.) In the old days, Twelfth Night marked the end of the religious feast of Christmas and a return to secular concerns, usually kicked off with a carnival. In medieval England there was a royal court masque on Twelfth Night, politically so important that foreign ambassadors would bribe and intrigue for position at it. The humbler folk celebrated with a carnival starting with a beanfeast involving a cake with a bean baked in it. Whoever got the slice of cake with the bean was master of the revels. (As for Shakespeare's *Twelfth Night,* that doesn't have much to do with anything at all, but was merely from his Neil Simon phase, one of his comedies in which a male actor playing a female role was then disguised as a boy, ho hum.)

Anyway, Twelfth Night. Neither Ginger nor I care about that sort of thing—we threw out our tree, along with several of its lights and ornaments, during our post-New-Year's-Eve-party fight—but Mary of course is a goddam traditionalist all the way, so not only did she keep her tree until today but insisted I go over this afternoon to help her and the kids undecorate.

Naturally, Ginger was annoyed. "You don't see *me* running off to Lance, do you?"

"He didn't ask," I said. "Besides, Helena wouldn't like it."

"And *I* don't like it," Ginger said, narrowing her eyes. She looks trampy when she narrows her eyes like that; I made the mistake of saying so once, so now she narrows her eyes all the way through parties and as a result spills her drink a lot. Now, narrowing her eyes without ulterior motive, she said, "What it comes down to is, Mary needs a fella."

"Amen," I said.

And it's true, it couldn't be more true. Ginger's ex-husband, Lance, lives now with Helena, an assistant production manager at Time, Inc., whose ex-husband Barry more or less lives with the ex-wife of a psychiatrist named Terriman or Telliman or something. (Don't worry about these names; these people don't matter.)

Anyway, Ginger and Lance's kids live with Ginger and me; Helena and Barry's kids are with Helena and Lance; the psychiatrist's kids are with Barry and whatsername. The psychiatrist contributes support money and Barry takes up the slack; Barry contributes support money for Helena and her kids and Lance takes up the slack; Lance contributes support money for Ginger and the kids here, and I take up the slack. And I contribute support money for Mary and *my* kids. . . .

And there's the rub. Mary, as Ginger pointed out, doesn't have a fella. Her freelance photography work and the research jobs probably bring in on average a little less than Ginger's salary, which is nowhere near enough for the lifestyle we all seem to have acquired. So while everybody else in the world is supporting two half-households, which adds up to one household, which is just barely possible, *I* am supporting one and one-half households all by myself, I've been doing it for eleven months, and I'm drowning.

Which is why *The Christmas Book* is so important. It could solve my money problems for a year, maybe two years; long enough, in any case, for Mary to give up the idea that I'm coming back. Long enough for her to find a fella.

With Ginger, I live on West End Avenue near 70th Street; Mary and the kids live downtown, on West 17th Street between Sixth and Seventh avenues; a fairly decent neighborhood, very near the Village and with much the same charm, but at lower rents. Going off now to disrobe the tree, I wore the sweater Mary'd given me for Christmas, to placate her. (I've already told Ginger it was my kids who gave me the sweater, to placate *her*.)

The Christmas decorations on Mary's tree seemed more *accurate*, somehow. Does that make any sense? Christmases come and Christmases go, and over the years some of the old ornaments break or crumple or disappear, new ones are added, there's a slow organic change, a continuous gradual shifting, every year subtly different and yet always the same, so that when you hear the phrase "Christmas tree" there's always one proto-tree that comes into your mind, and the rest are merely imitation.

I had time to brood about this because I spent an hour looking at the tree before we ever got around to undressing it. Mary met me at the door with cocoa and the news that the kids wanted to play Mille Bornes first, because it was alleged to be best with four. Since I was the one who'd given Jennifer the game for Christmas, and since the card table and chairs were already set up in the living room, I couldn't very well say no, so we all traveled several thousand miles together, while from time to time I looked past Bryan's head at the tree, thinking how accurate it was.

Jennifer, my firstborn, is eleven, a savvy, skinny New York kid and an absolute shark at games. Fortunately she's also lucky, because she cares *intensely* about whether she wins or loses. Bryan, nine years old, has already differentiated in his mind between sports (which are important) and games (which don't matter), so that's also good. Since Jennifer needs to win, and Bryan doesn't care but does enjoy playing, they make a kind of better Lucy and Charlie Brown, without (I hope) the psychological damage always implicit in "Peanuts."

Jennifer won twice, then I won. (She'd gone eight hundred fifty miles without using any two-hundreds, a gamble that would have paid off *big* if I hadn't scrambled to a graceless any-way-at-all win.) There had been talk about playing only three games, but when Jennifer was defeated on the third she got a set expression around the mouth, shuffled the cards like a pro, and said, "Just one more."

Mary said, "I'm not sure how long Tom can stay."

"I've got time," I said airily, though I knew Ginger would already be pacing the floor on 70th Street. "I'll be delighted to whup you twice in a row," I told Jennifer, which made her grin like Clint Eastwood and hunker down to *play*. She won, too.

After that, we put the table and chairs away and finally took care of the tree. Removing a rough-edged white snowball with a pale blue manger scene indented into one side, remembering that it was one of the few ornaments I'd brought with me from my parents' home, making it almost the oldest part of the continuity, the accuracy, I tried to think how I might gracefully ask to take it with me now, but there seemed to be no way. Palm it, pocket it? No.

By the end of the operation, Mary and I were alone, it having occurred to the kids that putting ornaments in boxes was *work* and not *play*. Also, I think they're both sometimes uncomfortable around me these days, possibly because I'm uncomfortable around them. I have this feeling they're not mature enough to realize how mature *I* am.

I put the naked tree in the hall, to carry down to the street when I left, and returned to the living room to say my farewells. On hands and knees there Mary picked needles one by one out of the carpet. "Well," I said, "I guess I'm off."

Kneeling, she sat back on her haunches, her cupped hands in her lap filled with pine needles. "Tom," she said, "do you remember Jack Horton?"

"Sure," I said. About my age, skinny and worried-looking, he lives in the neighborhood;

we have mutual friends, we meet occasionally at parties, we've never been close.

"Sit down a minute," she said.

Reluctantly, I sat facing her in "my" chair.

"I ran into Jack Horton at Key Food this afternoon," Mary said, "and he put his hand on my breast." She touched her fingertips to the spot.

I was surprised, and said so: "Jack Horton? Doesn't sound like him."

"I know," she agreed. "It's because men know I'm alone now," she said. "It's happened before, I've told you about it."

"Yes, you have." And she has, four or five times in the last couple of months, and with increasing detail, it seems to me. And always described in the same manner: not angry or upset or offended or anything, just calmly interested in this phenomenon that when a woman isn't already with a man other men come around and start copping feels.

"Of course," she said, "he *pretended* he was just admiring my dalmatian pin."

That would be a free-form, black-and-white mosaic pin Bryan had found at some Arab junk jewelry place in the Village and had given Mary for Christmas, announcing the weird-shaped lumpy thing was a dalmatian, as in the Walt Disney movie. I said, "Well, maybe that's what he was doing."

"Oh, no," she said. "He made sure he rubbed his knuckles back and forth on my nipple, like this." She demonstrated, watching her own knuckles with absorption.

Mary's campaign to get me back does not, I'm happy to say, include dressing up "sexy." At this moment she was barefoot, wearing old jeans and a dark blue high-neck sweater. But we were married a long while, it wasn't physical disinterest that broke us up, and I don't need suggestive clothing to remind me who's inside there. Watching her watch herself rub her nipple, I said, "Uh, like that, huh? What did you say?"

Her hand returned to help the other hand hold pine needles. "Of course, I pretended not to notice," she said. "It's a good thing it wasn't hard, though, or who knows *what* he would have thought."

What *I* thought then was, *He's a fella, Mary, maybe he likes you, he's decent, why not follow through?* That was what I thought, but not at all what I could say. "He probably didn't mean it," I said. "You should have said something right then, he probably would have turned red with embarrassment."

"Oh, he meant it," she said. "It's because you're away."

"Speaking of that," I said, bright and casual. "Ginger and I are thinking more seriously about marriage now, so we'll both have to get divorces, of course."

"I don't think Lance would like that," Mary said.

"Why's that?"

"Because then he'd be free to marry Helena, and Lance doesn't want to marry Helena."

It had been a mistake to mention marriage;
all I'd been trying to do was change the subject, plus reinforce the notion that since she
and I were never never never going to get
back together, why didn't she catch a couple
of these passes or go to a few parties and *find
a fella?* But marriage is Mary's subject, as I
should have remembered.

Still pretending to talk about Ginger's ex,
she went on, "Lance is just playing hookey.
Helena's an afternoon movie to him, that's
all."

"I have to go now," I said, and came back
home to Ginger's reproaches, which I have fled
by coming into my office to "work."

Well, if I'm working, let's work. There are a
couple of magazine pieces aborning on this
desk, and galleys of *The Films of Jack Oakie* to
correct, but my mind is still all caught up in
The Christmas Book. Will Jack Rosenfarb take
it? There isn't much time; maybe I should
phone somebody else, make another appointment for next week just in case.

If I peddle it to somebody else, who should
that be? Hubert Van Driin? The editor-pub-
lisher for whom I did the Jack Oakie book,
Hubert Van Driin is an insane right wing psy-
chopath, and his company, Federalist Press, is
much smaller than Craig, Harry & Bourke,
but my Christmas idea just might connect
with the nostalgia side of him. I could prom-

ise a still photo from a Wilderness Family movie; surely *those* people have done at least one Christmas-in-the-cabin sequence. On the other hand, Hubert is RC, from the Torquemada branch, and he might well get all pop-eyed and incensed at the secular side of Christmas. Hard to know, hard to know.

Dear———:

In conjunction with the publishing company of Craig, Harry & Bourke, I am compiling a book about Christmas. This is not intended, either by the publisher or myself, to be merely another standard compilation of the over-familiar and the over-anthologized, i.e., Dickens, Dylan Thomas, " 'Twas the night . . . ," etc.

Christmas is many things to many people. The Christmas Book will reflect that, presenting the full panorama of western man's most popular and meaningful holiday in a colorful, carefully-prepared, seriously-intentioned volume which we confidently expect will find its way under most every Christmas tree in America in the years to come.

In addition to Christmas art through the ages, and such rare and unknown treats as Kipling's "Christmas in India," the publishers and I intend a strong contemporaneous flavor by actively seeking out original stories, essays, reminiscences or whatever from the major writers and thinkers

*of our time. Your name could hardly be left
off such a list, which is the reason for this
letter.*

The Christmas Book *will stand or fall not
on its cullings from the libraries of the
past but on the contributions from people
like yourself who will tell us what Christmas means today, in modern America. Fees
are negotiable, but would certainly com-
pare favorably with what you would expect
for any equivalent piece in today's market.*

*Since we intend to be in the stores this
autumn, our deadline for inclusion in* The
Christmas Book *must be no later than June
1st, although some small leeway might be
possible in a very few special cases. I hope
you find this concept as intriguing as we
do, and will be inspired to give us your
unique contribution to the literature of
Christmas. May I hear from you soon?*

Sincerely,

*Thomas J. Diskant
General Editor*

Monday, January 10th

ABSOLUTELY insane! No more than twenty minutes after I phoned to make my appointment to see Hubert Van Driin at his office this Wednesday morning, Jack Rosenfarb called to say Craig, Harry & Bourke was "interested."

A mingy word, that. A cheap, sneaky, self-protecting fake of a word. "Interested." Interest is like smoke; it may mean fire, or it may dissipate in the wind.

"There's a good deal of interest around the shop in your idea," is the way Jack put it. "But the feeling is, we'd like to see something on paper."

There's nothing an editor likes more than reading words he hasn't had to pay for. They'd *all* like to see something on paper. When I was first in New York. . . .

Ah. When I was first in New York, what a

wealth of things I did not know. Entire ency-
clopedias of awful truths were unknown to
me. What I brought with me to the big city
nineteen years ago was a truly awesome ignorance, a change of clothing, and the belief
that my memory of a pink-walled garage surrounded by snow in sunlight was the most
important thing on Earth.

That's not how I would have phrased it
then, of course. I knew I was a writer, I knew
that much, and I knew I'd grown up in a
small town in southern Vermont that was absolutely full to the brim with *reality*, and I felt
I could snare that reality in a net of words, a
great open-mesh net of all the words I'd ever
learned in Vermont, that net I would toss
with a masterly flick of the wrist over that
pink-walled garage, and pull the cord, and I'd
have it!

I think it worked, actually. I did office temporary work, and knocked out a few magazine
articles to pay the rent on the studio apartment on West 101st Street, and spent most of
my time hunched over the typewriter, putting
the words down while that pink wall stood
and gleamed in my imagination. Pink-walled
garage out behind Bill Brewsher's house, with
the white snow around it in the sunlight. We
got really good snow in Vermont, really white
and glistening, not like this trash around here.
Every time I thought about Bill, or Candy, or
Jack and Jim Reilly, or Agnes, or any of them,

I always saw them as bundled-up fevered darknesses in front of that shining wall.

The Pink Garage Gang was bought for two thousand five hundred dollars by the fifth publisher who saw it. Print order three thousand, no advertising, no publicity. No paperback sale, no foreign rights sale. No movie interest. From time to time they sent me royalty statements; the last one, eleven hundred dollars of the advance was still unearned.

By the time *The Pink Garage Gang* was published I was more or less making my living with my typewriter. No more novels, though. I actually didn't have any more novels in my brain, I was too busy. Then, a few years ago, back in Vermont, a Burlington & Northern freight locomotive that somebody had forgotten to turn off or something got loose all by itself one night and trundled at a few miles an hour all the way up the state to the Canadian border before it stopped. All by itself. You may have read about it in the paper. It was winter, and everybody was in bed asleep, and the locomotive rolled slowly by, going north. It went right through my town. It was a moonlit night, and a few people here and there in the state looked out their windows, holding a glass of warm milk in their hand, and they saw the dark bulk of the locomotive go by.

For a while, I thought about that. I smiled sometimes, and thought about the locomotive basting a seam up through Vermont. God, that novel was real to me. I could *see* it, I could see everything in it, I knew everything in the world about that story. It was all so clear and detailed, I can still remember so much of it, that every once in a while there's a split second when I think I wrote it.

Jan 10

Jack Rosenfarb
Craig, Harry & Bourke
745 3rd Ave.
New York, NY 10017

Dear Jack:

  As you recall from our conversation of last week, and your telephone call to me this morning, I have it in mind to do a large glossy gift-book anthology on the subject of Christmas. I would combine already existing literature and artwork on the subject with original material solicited from the most prestigious writers and artists of our day, a list to include such as Norman Mailer, Joyce Carol Oates, Andy Warhol, Jerzy Kosinski, LeRoy Nieman, Jules Feiffer and Robert Ludlum, among many others. I see my own function as general editor of this anthology, engaged both in selecting the materials from the past and negotiating with the contributors of the present. In my previous work, as you know, I have frequently acted as a compiler and interviewer, experience which will stand me in good stead in re The Christmas Book.

As I mentioned to you last week, I would very strongly want this book to appear this calendar year, early enough for the Christmas season. Because time is relatively short, and because you have expressed some doubt as to whether Craig, Harry & Bourke would be the right publisher for this project, I have made a preliminary discussion with someone from another house. My own feeling, however, is that The Christmas Book *would be given its most careful and conscientious presentation with you as its editor, so I hope we can shortly come to a meeting of minds.*

Yours,

Tom Diskant

Wednesday, January 12th

WHAT a day. My daughter Jennifer got mugged this morning, which may turn out to be a blessing in disguise. Well, no, I don't mean it that way, I just mean it caused me to postpone my meeting with Hubert Van Driin.

I was just about to leave for that meeting—in fact, I was tying my tie—when the phone rang and it was Mary, sounding more solemn than usual (she's often serious, seldom solemn), saying, "Tom, could you come over right away?"

"Gee, I'm sorry, Mary," I said. "I'm just off to a meeting at Federalist Press."

"Couldn't you cancel it? I wouldn't ask, but Jennifer was mugged on her way to school."

So I canceled, of course. Van Driin took it well, with his normal reaction to the world we live in: "The barbarians are among us, Tom.

They came through the gates a long time ago, the liberals just waved the bastards in. Animals. The Duke knew."

"I'll call you later," I said, and left the apartment, and went down to 17th Street, where I found Mary and Jennifer in the kitchen, both bravely not having hysterics.

My kids go to public school because that's all I can afford. (That Ginger's kids go to private school, at Lance's expense, is an unstated bone of contention between Mary and me, *never* mentioned.) Bryan had sixty cents taken from him at school last year, which technically counts as a mugging though he wasn't harmed or actually threatened in any way, but this was Jennifer's first experience of street crime. Both the kids know enough not to offer resistance if you are outweighed, out-meaned or outnumbered; still, an assault for money is a tough experience for any person, and particularly so for an essentially nonviolent kid, as both of mine are.

Upon arrival, I crossed the kitchen to where mother and daughter sat at the table, and went down on one knee beside Jennifer's chair, resting my hand on her upper arm, saying, "How are you, tiger?"

She tried a smile, but her voice was shaky when she said, "I'm okay now."

"There was a knife," Mary said.

"Oh, Jesus," I said, and clasped her arm harder. "You weren't cut, were you? You weren't—"

"No, they just. . . ." She shook her head, frowned at her mother as though bewildered by some stray thought, then said, "He just had it in his hand. He didn't even say anything, he just held the knife up and showed it to me and grinned real mean, and the other one said gimme your money."

"Two of them? Older boys?"

"Grown-up, kind of," she said. "Like you see playing basketball."

"Twenty year olds," Mary translated.

I could feel Jennifer's skinny arm trembling, like when you hold a frightened cat. She said, "I just thought, oh, wow, what if I don't have enough for them? Enough money, I mean, I only had, I. . . ." Her face scrinched up. "Ohh," she said, on a rising note.

Then at last she dissolved, and I held her very close, and Mary came over to pat us both on the shoulder. I sat on the floor, pulling Jennifer down onto my lap, curling her in against me there, rocking back and forth and holding her while she cried herself out. I said stupid things like, "There, there," and "It's all right now," and, "Okay, okay." Mary made coffee for herself and me and Earl Grey tea for Jennifer, who doesn't like coffee, and after a while we got off the floor and sat around the kitchen table instead and drank our stimulants and Jennifer went about reconstructing her public persona as the hip existential city kid. "It was all such a complete drag," she said. "I had to tell the cops they were *black* guys, it was like I was making it up, you know? An agent provocataer. And one of the cops was black, so it was really embarrassing."

I love both my kids, with a mad helpless mute mortifying love that gets more bumble-footed the stronger I feel it or the harder I try to express it. Realizing Jennifer already had too much to bend her mind around at the moment, I mostly kept quiet, so she wouldn't also have to deal with her father's inadequacies. "The black cops know," was all I said at that juncture.

She managed a little grin, a condensed version of her usual mode. "He looked real tough," she said. "I bet if *he* caught those guys, he'd beat them up a lot worse than a white cop, wouldn't he?"

"Maybe so," I said, smiling back.

Mary said, "Jennifer's staying home from school today, I phoned the school and they know about it. Tom, why don't you stay and have lunch with us?"

"Let me take you both *out* to lunch."

Mary had to drape herself in cameras before we left, which used to annoy me toward the end of our marriage but which I now am becoming indulgent about again, as I had been when first we'd met. Mary, out of East St. Louis, had come to New York originally to be a photographer, having won some awards and sold some pictures at the local or regional level. When I first met her, at a magazine's Christmas party, she was making a precari-

ous living doing freelance research for everybody and anybody: museums, book illustrators,
ad agencies. She would root around in libraries and morgues and find you just the right
daguerreotype to go with your pantyhose ad,
or the eleven specific paintings ripping off (or
"homaging") such-and-such a Rembrandt, or
clear photos of every kind of European tram
at the turn of the century, or whatever you
want. Meantime, she was taking millions of
pictures of her own, submitting them everywhere, looking for an agent, and hoping for
the best.

Which never came. We married, we had the
kids, she continued the research work to sup-
plement my income, and she went on taking
pictures, but very few have been published.

The problem is, she doesn't have a unique
eye. Although she's always surrounded herself
with hung copies of Diane Arbus photos, for
instance, she herself has a much softer, more
sympathetic view of the world, and could never
look through her lens as dispassionately as
Arbus. On the other hand, she has too much
sophistication and self-awareness to go for
"pretty" pictures, calendar art, so her work is
stuck somewhere in the middle: too knowing
to be sentimental, too gentle to be striking.

It used to bother me that she couldn't go
anywhere without the cameras, because I knew
she was just kidding herself and wasting her
time, but now that we're apart she's no longer
my problem, and I can see photography as

merely Mary's hobby. (If Mary herself ever heard me use the word "hobby" in that context, she would take a gun and shoot me. No fooling.)

So, with pauses for Mary to take pictures of interesting gutter-rubbish and amusing company names on truck sides, we walked down into the Village and had cheeseburgers in a joint where we could watch the trucks thunder down Seventh Avenue and I could have a Bloody Mary. My Mary had coffee, and Jennifer had iced tea. The waitress stared at her, stared at January outside the window, and said, "*Iced* tea?"

"The cheeseburger's hot," Jennifer pointed out. "And my father's Bloody Mary is cold."

By the time lunch was over and we'd walked back up to 17th Street Jennifer had sufficiently rewritten history in her own mind as to believe she'd never actually lost her cool through the whole experience. That belief was by now the most important part of it for her, much more important than the lost dollar-eighty or the capturing of the punks that did it. When, as we turned off Seventh Avenue, she said, "I figured, just so *they* didn't panic, I was probably okay," I knew the healing process was well under way. What a terrific kid; tough and hip, like her old man.

Mary invited me upstairs, but I said I had things to do. Jennifer said, "Thanks for coming down."

"Hey," I said, "what's a father for? Don't answer that."

We kissed, and she said, "*You're* okay."

"Here's looking at *you*, kid."

Mary kissed my cheek and looked deeply in my eyes and I came back uptown where Jack Rosenfarb's voice greeted me on the answering machine, saying, "Tom, please call me. Got your letter, thought I had an exclusive on this. Give me a ring as soon as you can." The unsettled sound in his voice was music to my ears.

So I gave him a ring and he said, "Tom, you're not putting me in a bid situation, are you?"

"Of course not," I said. There is nothing I would love more than to have two heavyweight publishers bidding for my idea, but since I can't figure out how to arrange such a scenario I might as well claim the high moral principle: "I wouldn't do a thing like that."

"Well, what's with this 'preliminary discussion'?" He sounded actually aggrieved. "At lunch, you said I was the only one you were talking to."

"That's true," I said. "It was true last week, but you really didn't sound that enthusiastic, Jack, not at lunch and not on the phone Monday. You know, talking about my track record and all that. And the time factor is—"

"Tom, *I* was enthusiastic! But I had to be sure the company would back me up. Tom, you don't know what an editor has to go

48   *Donald E. Westlake*

through, they second-guess my judgment all
the time, I could wind up with egg on my
face, trouble with— Well. You don't want to
know my problems," he said accurately.

"Jack," I said, "I'm sorry if you feel I've
behaved in an underhanded way or anything
like that. The instant I spoke to another—"

"You told me about it, I know that, I know
that. Just between you and me, who are you
talking to?"

If I were to answer *Hubert Van Driin*, Jack
might merely laugh and hang up, so I said, "I
probably shouldn't say, Jack. I haven't told
him your name either, but I've been just as
upfront with—"

"I know you, Tom," he said hurriedly, "you
don't have to tell me all that, you're an honorable fellow, I know that. All right. You want
this thing to move fast, I don't blame you for
that, so the instant I got your letter I took it
to Wilson, and *he* took it to Bourke, and assuming we can work out the money, we're
interested."

"Interested?"

"We want to do the book!"

That was so terrific I just blurted out the
first thing that came into my mind: "That's
terrific!"

"Yeah," he said, a bit sourly. They hate to
be rushed, editors, they're cowlike in several
ways, including being my source of milk. Anyway, he said, "All we have to do is come to a
meeting of minds about the money."

"I'll call Annie," I said, "and have her call you."

"Good. But one thing, about this other house you were talking to. Tom, I have to tell you, we won't get into a bidding war, and that's flat."

Oh, yes, you would, I thought, if I only knew how to set one up. "Don't worry, Jack," I told him. "As of this minute, they're out."

We exchanged one or two ritual coins of mutual esteem, and then I phoned Annie, who was in the office and taking calls. "Did you phone me?" she demanded, her ancient voice querulous and short-tempered.

"I'm phoning you *now*," I said.

"In the last day or two. And not leave any message."

"Me, Annie? I know how you feel about that."

"Somebody's been— Well, never mind. What can I do for you, Tom?"

I was glad it was one of her good days; on the bad days she calls me Tim. Succinctly I described my book idea, my negotiations with Jack, and the current situation. She listened, with occasional grunts, then said, "I don't get it. What kinda book is this?"

I told her again. She said, "Everybody's idle thoughts about Christmas."

"Every *famous* body's idle thoughts about Christmas."

"If you give *me* one of those books next Yuletide," she said, "I'll fling it in your face."

"Annie, you inspire me."

"As I understand the situation," she said, "you have now placed me in the position of agenting for the entire western literary world, all at once."

"Don't forget the artists."

"*And* the artists. I'll call Jack Rosenfarb and find out if he's really fallen for this one."

"Thank you, Annie."

"You'll hear from me," she said vaguely, and hung up.

So the only question left is, what idea am I going to peddle to Hubert Van Driin?

Friday, January 14th

SO here's their opening offer, and even as an opening offer it stinks. Five thousand dollars on signature, twenty thousand when I have commitments from five "individuals mutually agreed to be prominent," and another twenty-five thousand on August first. If I don't have those five prominent noses by June first the deal is off.

Out of this lavish fifty thou, I'm supposed to pay all the contributors! (There's an additional five thousand they've agreed to pay for "research and secretarial" expenses, upon receipt of receipts.) And, as Jack himself pointed out, I'm not running a charity here, I do want a little something for myself.

One good thing about Annie; she's *involved*. When she saw Craig's insulting offer, she smiled thinly and decided to get serious. Annie, who began in publishing as somebody's secretary during the Adams administration—the elder Adams—and who apparently in her youth screwed most of the literate men on the Eastern Seaboard, has aged into a scrawny bad-tempered old buzzard who knows everybody, loves to fight and has been known to get blood from a stone simply by squeezing hard enough. What can be done, Annie will do.

On the home front, Ginger is very up and positive about *The Christmas Book* and is saying maybe we can take a winter vacation after all. (Last year we did a week at a condominium on St. Croix, splitting the cost, but this year money has been tighter for both of us.) Ginger's eight-year-old daughter, Gretchen, is also excited and is doing me watercolors of Christmas scenes "for the book." She's a nice kid, Gretchen, and if it's possible to say that an eight-year-old is talented, Gretchen is probably talented along graphic arts lines—maybe someday she'll go to the High School of Art and Design—but I'm getting a little tired of primitive Nativity scenes and Santa Claus getting out of taxis and all this stuff. I hope and expect that boredom will set in soon—on her part, I'm already bored—and save me.

Ginger is also being active on the project, but in a more useful way. She's copy editor at Trans-American Books, a paperback house, and is a very good line editor; she's rewritten my solicitation letter—the one to be sent to prominent noses—and I have to admit she was right with most of the changes she suggested.

For instance, she pointed out that it wasn't until the third paragraph that I got to the point of the letter, asking for original material. "Until then," she said, "it sounds like you're trying to sell them a copy of the book." So now, with some necessary adaptation, the third paragraph is the second and the second is the third.

Also, with Ginger's help, I did a variant letter aimed at photographers, illustrators and graphic artists. (Other than Gretchen.) I'm hoping they'll be cheaper than the writers.

The question is, when do I actually get to send out these letters?

Wednesday, January 19th

A full week of negotiation, and I am not entirely happy at the result, but Annie says it's the best we can do, and too late to try any other house this year, so this morning we said yes and Jack Rosenfarb messengered to Annie's office a letter of intent outlining the agreement; that was so I could get started without waiting for contracts to be drawn.

Anyway, the deal. I get twenty-five thousand on signature, another twenty-five June first (dependent on yesses from those five celebs), and the rest August first. The full advance is on a sliding scale between seventy-five and one hundred twenty-five thousand dollars, with sixty percent going to the contributors and forty percent to me.

And, if the deal falls through, five thousand of the first advance is mine anyway, to pay for my time and effort. So no matter *what* happens, this idea has at least earned me five grand.

Annie, whose office is a janitor's closet on a low floor of the Empire State Building, took me to lunch in her neighborhood and gave me a copy of Jack Rosenfarb's letter, and I actually saw her smile a bit. She had a Jack Daniel's and two glasses of white wine and became vague toward the end of the meal, calling me "Tim" and saying sentences that almost seemed coherent until you looked back at them. For instance, she allowed as how she'd been warming to the idea of *The Christmas Book* over the last week or so, from her initial negative reaction, and by now was quite fond of the notion. "The best books, like the best women, are all whores," she went on. "Never trust an amateur at anything."

"Okay," I said.

I walked her back to her office, happy she wouldn't be doing anything on *my* career's behalf this afternoon, and then came home to start work. Yesterday Ginger ran off on the Xerox machine at work a hundred copies of my two solicitation letters, with a blank for me to type in the victim's name, so I have just sent the writer's letter to these forty people:

Edward Albee, Woody Allen, Isaac Asimov, Russell Baker, Ann Beattie, Helen Gurley Brown, William F. Buckley, Jr., Leo Buscaglia, Truman Capote, Jimmy Carter, Francis Ford Coppola, Annie Dillard, E. L. Doctorow, Gerald Ford, William Goldman, John Irving, Stephen King, Jerzy Kosinski, Judith Krantz, Robert Ludlum, Norman Mailer, James A. Michener, Daniel Patrick Moynihan, Richard Nixon, Joyce Carol Oates, Mario Puzo, Joan Rivers, Andy Rooney, Philip Roth, Carl Sagan, Isaac Bashevis Singer (what the hell), Steven Spielberg, Sylvester Stallone, Diana Trilling, John Updike, Gore Vidal, Kurt Vonnegut, Joseph Wambaugh, Tom Wolfe and Herman Wouk.

The illustrator's letter went to these ten people:

Charles Addams, Richard Avedon, Jim Davis, Jules Feiffer, Edward Gorey, Robert Kliban, Jill Krementz, LeRoy Nieman, Charles Schulz and Andy Warhol.

I was just typing *Carl Sagan* when Hubert Van Driin called to say he thought we'd had a nice and productive chat on Monday, but on reflection he was deciding to say no to *The Wit and Wisdom of Clint Eastwood*. It's probably just as well.

Monday, February 7th

BACK to a blizzard. It took *three hours* to get home from Kennedy Airport last night, during which Ginger and I finally had the big fight that had been brewing all week in Puerto Rico, and the cabdriver *took her side*! The son of a bitch. With the two of them ganging up on me, I gathered my dignity like the tattered cloak it is, stepped out into the storm, and swore to walk home.

Well, I stomped through the snow and the wind and the stalled traffic and the slush on the Van Wyck Expressway for about two minutes before realizing I could die out there, which was carrying hurt pride too far, so I went back to the cab—which, of course, hadn't moved an inch while I was away—to find Ginger arguing with the *driver*. Hah-*hah*! I sat in my corner, silent, arms folded, a superior

smile on my triumphant face while they squab-
bled, and my feet, in wet socks, slowly turned
to marble and fell off.

Eventually the three of us made up, Ginger
explaining to the driver that it was just that I
was worried about money. I know her well
enough by now to understand that statement
as her form of apology. In changing the subject of the argument to something less vola-
tile and dangerous, she was in effect saying
she didn't want to argue any more.

While it is true that I'm worried about
money—we are spending Craig, Harry &
Bourke's advance before receiving it and without
regard for the fact that I'm going to have to
pay other people for contributions to the
book—in truth that wasn't what the fight was
about. The fight was about children, hers and
mine, but because that problem is too deli-
cate and insoluble to deal with directly we
tend just to gnaw at its fringes.

None of these kids is going to go away,
and all of them are going to live with their
mothers till they grow up, and this means
that more and more men are going to be surrounded by children they aren't to blame for.
Meanwhile, their own kids are eating popcorn
with other males. It all creates tension.

The specific of this fight was whether Ginger's kids should come back from Lance's right
away last night, as soon as we ourselves got
home, or should they come back today, after
school. The fight had been poised for birth

ever since the Saturday before last, when I took Gretchen and Joshua to their father's apartment to stay while Ginger and I were in Puerto Rico, but neither of us had wanted to spoil our departure—nor our vacation—so the dispute merely seethed and bubbled beneath the surface, present but not active. The image of a volcano seems appropriate. Returning to New York amid a snowstorm and a monumental traffic tie-up had at last given the fight a soil in which it could grow (to mix my imagery just a teeny bit), and thus it all came about.

(What Ginger fought with the cabdriver about was Puerto Rico, he being an emigrant from there.)

That the rotten weather made the whole question of the kids' return academic merely gave the fight added virulence. We would be lucky to get *ourselves* home on Sunday night, never mind the kids. Since I had been the one pressing the point of view that a brief overnight transition for the two of us between traveling and children would be a good idea, I was accused in the taxi of gloating over the storm, and off we went.

Well, it all calmed down en route, though it did threaten to blow up all over again when two of the messages awaiting us on the telephone answering machine at home were from Mary, and both about *her* kids. That is, our kids. Bryan having been given a clarinet for Christmas—don't ask me why kids want this or that, I'll never fathom it—(a used clarinet from a pawnshop on Third Avenue), it now seemed a potentially good idea to give him clarinet lessons, so one of Mary's calls was about the thirty-five-dollar-a-month lessons available through the school. The other message was about the police wanting Jennifer to make a statement about her mugging, and did I think it was a good idea for the kid to involve herself in all that any further.

Ginger's nostrils were flaring by that point, and she'd narrowed her eyes so much she looked like a leftover alien from *Star Wars*. We could have had round two of the day if the calls hadn't annoyed me just as much as they did her. Mary had known I was in Puerto Rico, she knew when I was coming back, and dropping those two "innocent" messages on the machine was just another way to turn the knife of pseudodomesticity. I expressed that opinion aloud, Ginger's eyes and nose returned to their accustomed shapes, and we went to bed to have the kind of sex that makes it all worthwhile, as outside the storm raged unabated.

None of the other answering machine messages had been of much import, but when I finally got to the mail this morning there were seven responses to my solicitation for *The Christmas Book*, and I don't know if I'm encouraged or not.

Two of the letters, from Diana Trilling and Andy Rooney, merely asked, in one way or another, how much I was offering to pay. In fact, Andy Rooney's letter, in toto, said, "Dear Mr. Diskant, How much? Yours, Andrew A. Rooney." Now, that's what I call a few words from Andy Rooney!

But it wasn't the shortest letter. That came from Joan Rivers, and it went:

January 25

Dear Thomas J. Diskant:

What?

Joan Rivers

The longest response came from a literary agent named Scott Meredith, and for quite a while I couldn't figure out what was going on. It was a box, a big manuscript box about twice the normal depth, absolutely crammed full with manuscripts of short stories and articles and poetry. Some of the pieces seemed fairly recent, others were on yellowed dog-eared paper with various stains, but all of them, by golly, were on the subject of Christmas.

A letter from Scott Meredith had come with this armada of failed hopes, and in it Meredith explained that he was Norman Mailer's agent, that Mailer might be interested in doing a small piece for *The Christmas Book* if the price were right, and in the meantime these other works by "outstanding writers, clients of mine" were probably right down my alley.

No. Definitely not.

The remaining three responses were also loony, each in its own way. Stephen King wrote a long enthusiastic sloppy letter saying *The Christmas Book* was a wonderful idea and he'd love to do something for it if he could think of something, and in the meantime he had these suggestions of other absolutely wonderful things I ought to put in the book, like "Death On Christmas Eve" by Stanley Ellin and "Christmas Party" by Rex Stout, and on and on.

From Jimmy Carter I got permission to do the book, I think. I'm not sure what his letter was, some sort of proclamation about the good and worthy work I was undertaking, but I began to believe he failed to understand the thrust of my original letter. (Or whoever actually answered it did.) And from Charles Schulz I got, in triplicate, a contract I was to sign which made it clear that I would not participate in any subsidiary rights to anything by him or about him or any character created by him that might appear in *The Christmas Book* or its promotion or advertising. Sheesh!

So. I dropped lines to Trilling and Rooney saying I would pay "in the neighborhood of" a thousand dollars for a thousand words. I sent a note to King thanking him for all his suggestions and adding that what I was really looking forward to was his own original contribution to *The Christmas Book*. I wrote Carter that I hoped he could see his way toward contributing some personal thoughts on the subject of Christmas, and I penned a missive to Rivers saying that since she had dealt with motherhood twice, in her movie *Rabbit Test* and her book *Having A Baby Can Be A Scream*, maybe she had a stray thought or two about Christmas as well, and would she be willing to share it? I phoned the Scott Meredith Agency to request a messenger to come pick up these huddled masses they'd sent me, and included in the package a note describing my thousand dollar neighborhood, for Mailer's consideration. Schulz's contract I sent to Jack Rosenfarb, with a note saying, "You'll probably know what to do with this."

Next, feeling virtuous from all my activity, I phoned Mary, who worked very hard at being a downer; not like her, but I think she was annoyed both by winter and by my having been away from it for a week. She said things like, "Bryan needs to see more of you," and, "I think Jennifer feels the lack of a father particularly at this time, after the mugging," and so on. I handled it well for a while, and then I didn't handle it well at all, and then I hung up.

While in Puerto Rico I'd thought of some more famous people I should hit on, so after the emotional upset of the Mary call I soothed myself by sending the writer's letter to ten more possibles: Arthur C. Clarke, Joan Didion, John Gregory Dunne, John Kenneth Galbraith, Garrison Keillor, Henry Kissinger, Jonathan

Schell, Mickey Spillane, William Styron and
Paul Theroux. Plus the illustrator's letter to
these five: Roddy McDowall, Helmut Newton,
Francesco Scavullo, Gahan Wilson and Jamie
Wyeth.

Lance just called. Gretchen and Joshua have
arrived at his place from school, and he wants
me to come get them. The storm continues,
that's why; if the weather were decent, he'd
cab them across town himself. Selfish bastard.

Sunday, February 13th

ONE of the reasons people are always more complicated than you expect them to be is that they are always sillier than you expect them to be. Take holidays, anniversaries, birthdays and special occasions in general. In the course of any given year, each of us has to remember and deal appropriately with not only all the great public occasions—Easter, Thanksgiving, the Fourth of July, my current meal ticket Christmas, and all the rest—but with the proliferating private events as well. As families separate and reshuffle themselves and regroup in new combinations, there are more and more birthdays to remember, more and more anniversaries to acknowledge, more and more special occasions to commemorate.

But separation itself? Isn't that going too far? Now I have found out why Mary was so bad-tempered last week and why she put those two irritating messages on the answering machine while Ginger and I were away. It was because I was in Puerto Rico on February third.

February third? What, you wonder, is February third, that it should have such importance, that if we were Hispanic we would name a plaza for it? It is the date, last year, that I packed two suitcases and a liquor store carton and moved from downtown to uptown, thus ending my marriage and going public with Ginger. My crime this year is that I did not acknowledge the first anniversary of that momentous occasion, was not even present with Mary to—celebrate? mourn? remember? reaffirm?—and therefore she got mad.

It took her a while to say so; until today, in fact, when I brought the kids back from their weekend with Daddy. She had still been cold and rather nasty yesterday morning when I picked them up—rather like the weather—but today she had changed back to her normal self, which is both patient and insidious. As the kids went off to their room to unbundle, Mary said, "Have a cup of coffee, you look cold."

I was, but I said, "I ought to get back uptown."

"It's already made," she said, and because I could see the irritability had departed (a trend I want to encourage) I said fine, and we sat together in the kitchen over coffee and Entenmann's pound cake. We talked about the kids for a while—it turns out Jennifer doesn't have to involve herself with the police any more, after all—and then Mary said, "Why did you choose that particular time to go to Puerto Rico?"

"You mean winter?"

"I mean that week."

"That was when Ginger could get off from work," I said. I hadn't the slightest idea where the conversation was going.

"No other reason?"

"What other reason is there?"

"February third?"

I looked at her, shaking my head, waiting for her to go on, while she leaned forward slightly, gazing at me in an expectant *testing* kind of way. Then she leaned back, relaxing, shaking her head, saying, "You don't remember."

"February third." I frowned, casting my mind back. "Good God, is that when— Let's see, the third was a Thursday this year, so it would have been Wednesday last—"

Then it came to me. That was the date all right, that was the moment when seven months of distress and trouble and finagling and sneaking around had finally come to a head and I had at last broken out of this cocoon, or egg, or whatever it was.

It all began the summer before last, part of which we spent in a rented house on Fire Island, where I was one of the few males who didn't commute daily or weekly to a job in the city. Mary and I had been drifting apart—at any rate *I* had been drifting apart—and either there were more targets of opportunity among the solitary daytime wives that summer or I was in a mood to be more aware of them; whatever the reason, I took my opportunities where I found them, feeling both pleased with myself and guilty, until I realized Mary knew what was going on and did not ever plan to say a word about it.

That was the finish. Of everything, ultimately, but initially it was the finish of both the pleasure *and* the guilt. I think I could have stood anything else from Mary: raging arguments, brokenhearted pleas, stern admonitions, her own revenge infidelities, you name it. But to be *humored*, to matter that little, took the starch out of more than my sails. There was no more catting around that summer, but one evening when we were alone for dinner—both kids "eating over" with friends, as the local argot had it—I broke a buzzing long silence by saying, "Mary, this marriage is over."

She looked at me calmly. "No, it isn't, Tom," she said.

"Oh, yes, it is."

"You're just resisting being a grown-up," she said. "You want one more round before the bars close."

One last fling. The seven year itch. The last hurrah. All that easy dismissal. "Mary," I said, "you are reducing me to Dagwood Bumstead, and *that's* why this marriage is over."

But it wasn't over that moment, or that easily. We continued to live together, and in the fall I started up with Ginger, who over the summer had broken up with Lance. (We'd met the Patchetts several years before, and had become friends.) Maybe in my summertime flings I'd been trying to attract Mary's attention, I'm not sure about that, but when I took up with Ginger I made damn sure there'd be no chance for Mary to do her shrinking head act again. I was sly, I was slippery, I was plausible, and I was *not found out*. Ginger and I originally got together in October, and by late November we both knew we could have a long-term thing together if we wanted. But families don't break up before Christmas, so we waited.

Pre-Christmas shopping is, of course, the perfect cover for the adulterer. We're all off on mysterious errands all the time anyway. But then Christmas itself is a downer, if you know you're about to pack up and leave this crowd gathered happily around this tree, which may be why I stalled and dawdled all the way through January, until Ginger asked me straight out whether I was going to leave my wife, "because if you aren't, you're going to leave *me*. I won't play *Back Street*, Tom."

So that's when I did it. February third, the anniversary of which I had been so unfeeling as to forget. Nodding at Mary, in her kitchen, I said, "That's when I left."

She offered a sad smile and said, "I had been hoping it was when you would come back."

"Mary," I said.

She raised her hand to stop me. "I know, we just keep saying the same things over and over again. I hope you'll come back, you hope you won't."

"I know I won't."

"I'll wait," she said.

"I wish you wouldn't. And there's no point remembering that date any more, it doesn't mean anything."

"I'll remember it anyway," she said, and smiled.

~~~~~~~~~~~~~~~~

Tuesday, February 15th

WHY do I let Mary sucker me this way? I just get hell afterwards from Ginger.

Yesterday was Valentine's Day. My attitude toward holidays generally is that they are a terrible interruption in the life of a freelancer—nobody's around in any of the offices to answer my calls—and my attitude toward Valentine's Day in particular is that it's on a par with having a feast day for coronary thrombosis. Don't people realize the awful harm done by romance? All those cutesy red valentine hearts should be edged in black. "Be my valentine," is an insidious sentence to teach a child. (As with most general festive occasions, we busy adults have also left this one to be observed by our children.)

The whole thing is a ghastly mistake anyway. St. Valentine, if there ever was a St.

Valentine, had nothing to do with hearts or romance or Hallmark Cards. Way back when, there may actually have been two priests named Valentine, both martyred during the reign of the emperor Claudius—and he seemed such a nice fellow on television, too—or the two stories may refer to the same ill-treated priest, or he may just be a legend after all, like St. Christopher. The point is, his feast day on February fourteenth has to do with *martyrdom,* not love and sex; or am I missing something here?

Anyway, apparently St. Valentine's remembrance day got mixed up somewhere along the line with a Roman festival called Lupercalia on February fifteenth, one day later, which was itself pretty weird. The Luperci were a group of priests who, every February fifteenth, would start the day by sacrificing some goats and a dog. (There was no particular god or goddess they were sacrificing to, this was just something they did.) Then they cut lengths of thong from the skins of the sacrificed goats and ran naked around the walls of the Palatine the rest of the day, hitting people with the thongs.

All of this was more necromancy than religion, an occult act that was supposed to make a magic ring around the city, keeping good luck inside and bad luck out. And (this may at last be where the modern Valentine's Day idea got started) being hit by one of those thongs

on that particular day was supposed to cure
sterility.

(A kind of fresh pork sausage with ground
pignoli nuts, cumin seed, bay leaves and black
pepper was eaten that day, as part of the
ritual, and became so identified with Lupercalia that when the emperor Constantine
turned Christian he banned the eating of sausage, which of course immediately created a
whole army of sausage bootleggers, and may
explain why Al Capone always looked like a
sausage.)

In any event, Mary phoned yesterday afternoon to say I should come to dinner because
Jennifer had returned from school distraught
that she hadn't received *enough* Valentine cards
and was therefore humiliated with her peer
group.

"Enough? What do you mean enough? How
many sexual propositions is a decent eleven-
year-old girl supposed to receive in one day?"

"Sex has nothing to do with it, Tom," Mary
said, "as you very well know. Valentines have
to do with popularity and friendship."

"It's a holiday in honor of lust, that's what
it is," I insisted. "One of the seven deadly
sins, commemorated. *And* named after a saint."

"Stop being silly, Tom. Jennifer needs you."

So I went, of course, and Jennifer didn't
really need me, of course, it was all simply
another part of Mary's doomed campaign to
recapture me, which I told her over coffee, at
the end of the meal, after the kids had gone

into the living room to watch television. "Jennifer's fine," I said accusingly.

"Yes," she said, deliberately misunderstanding. "You helped a great deal, Tom."

"I didn't help at all. There was nothing to help *about*."

"Jennifer always keeps a stiff upper lip when you're around," she told me. "She knows you like it."

It was time—past time—to change the subject. "Well," I said, staring wildly around the kitchen in search of subject matter, "I see the super finally fixed that broken shelf."

"He sent a carpenter," she said.

"A real one? Good."

"A great big tall man," she said, "with tattoos on his arms."

"Ah."

"Emilio must have told him I was living alone," she said, Emilio being the super.

Why didn't I see it coming? Nevertheless, I didn't. "Oh?" I said. "Why's that?"

"He kept being *very* suggestive."

"Oh, come on, Mary, you're just imagining—"

"Oh, no, I'm not," she said. "He kept looking at my body, you know the way I mean? And then he'd stroke his hammer like this." Her hand made an *O* and stroked a nonexistent something, possibly a hammer.

"No," I said. "While hammering *nails*? He couldn't."

"He had a big tool belt, you know," she told

me, "slung low around his hips like in westerns."

"Gun belts."

"That's right. The hammer was in a loop on the side, hanging down, and he kept turning sideways and holding the hammer out so it looked like it was between his legs, and then he'd look at my body and stroke the hammer like this." And she did that movement again.

The worst of it was her calmness. If she'd been upset, or frightened, or outraged, or even turned on by it all, I could have handled the problem—dealt with the problem, I mean—calmly and reassuringly, from my more experienced masculine perspective. But *she* was the calm one, which left me . . . I don't know where it left me. Despite myself, knowing it could only get worse, I said, "Did he, uh. . . . He didn't *say* anything, did he? It was probably just an unconscious gesture."

"I offered him some coffee," she said, "and he asked me if I had any jelly."

"Jelly?"

"I looked in the refrigerator, right there, and he was over here, and I bent down to look in the lower shelves, and when I looked back he was *staring* at me, and doing this with the hammer."

"Don't *do* that!"

"Well, I told him I had raspberry jelly, and strawberry jelly, you know, what the kids like, and he said, 'Don't you have any other kind of jelly?' and I said, 'No,' and he said, 'I sure do like jelly, I like to lick it all up,' and then he did this again."

"I have to go now," I said, and came back to my own valentine, who had been having a telephonic fight with Lance about money. It was moot for a while as to whether Ginger would now transfer the fight to *me*, as being another sonofabitch male, or would become very warm and loving and sexy with me, as revenge against her husband; fortunately, the latter impulse won.

As for *The Christmas Book*, that continues apace. I have actually received three submissions, one of which I unfortunately had to reject:

Dear John Irving,

"The Stars Wink," your short-short story about a bear whose eyes are put out by feminists on Christmas Eve, is certainly a powerful piece of writing, right up there with the rest of your work, and I for one would be proud indeed to publish it under any circumstance at all. Unfortunately, I don't always have final say on these matters, and the feeling at Craig, Harry & Bourke was that the date of Christmas Eve in the story was merely happenstantial (apparently typed in later once or twice, in fact), that the story had very little to say about Christmas qua Christmas, and that all in all the tale was rather more depressing than we prefer for the contents of The Christmas

Book. *Your suggestion that Tomi Ungerer illustrate your story would be an excellent one were we to publish the story, except that we already have approached Mr. Ungerer to do something rather different and more Yulesque.*

Otherwise, Isaac Asimov's piece about the aerodynamic qualities of Santa's sleigh, and Andy Rooney's piece about how there weren't all these different sized batteries when he was a child, were both slight but puckish, and I was pleased to take them. That is, I've sent them on to Jack Rosenfarb for approval and payment, and have no doubt he'll accept them.

"How much?" letters have now been received from Russell Baker, William F. Buckley, Jr., Truman Capote, Carl Sagan and Kurt Vonnegut, and have been answered. And *this* came from Mario Puzo's secretary:

Mr. Puzo has asked me to tell you that he is tired of people trying to capitalize on his alleged relationship with the Mafia. He has not the slightest interest in writing about the Mafia's view of Christmas, nor if he did have such an interest would he be willing to share his thoughts with you.

Well, I just sent him the regular form letter, didn't I? I never *mentioned* the Mafia! Enraged, I sat at my typewriter and wrote:

Dear Mr. Puzo:

Thank you for your prompt response to my query letter concerning The Christmas Book. *If you have nothing at the moment about the Mafia vis-a-vis Christmas, perhaps you'd like to give us a few words on Christmas in Las Vegas (though we do have a shot at Carol Doda on that topic), or maybe even a thinkpiece on the Christmas presents exchanged by Superman and Lois Lane. Or it could be you have in the trunk something about Easter or the Fourth of July that could be adapted. Looking forward to your response.*

Well, I didn't send that letter, of course; Puzo's name would be damn useful in the book. A bit later, calmer, I wrote a letter apologizing for having created the misunderstanding and assuring Mr. Puzo I had no thought of confining his creativity in re Christmas to any specific area; *anything* at all about Christmas, honest (except blind bears, I didn't add).

And just to make life complete, today I got Scott Meredith's dead-bone collection again! It seems Arthur C. Clarke is a client of his. "Oh, was that you?" said a female voice there when I phoned them to re-send their messenger.

I have now sent the solicitation letter to five more writers—Pauline Kael, John Leonard, Sam Shepard, John Simon and Calvin

Trillin—and five more artists—Jasper Johns,
David Levine, Roy Lichtenstein, Saul Steinberg
and Tomi Ungerer. I back-dated the Ungerer
letter.

~~~~~~~~~~~~~~~~~~~~~~~

Monday, March 21st

DISASTER! Jack Rosenfarb QUIT this morning!
This is the worst thing that can happen in the publishing industry, bar none. It is worse than a bad dust jacket or a low ad budget or even another book on the same subject coming out two months ahead. It is *much* worse than a libel suit or a *Publishers Weekly* slam or a paperback auction to which nobody comes.

Here's the problem. Your average publishing company is the last existing model of the feudal system at (semi)work. Every department is its own fiefdom, jealous of its windows and its telephones and its supplies of paper clips. No one is in overall charge, no one. Publishers themselves have nothing whatsoever to do with books—would you expect Mr. Standard to hang out with his toilets? —and what the hell do employees care?

Publishing is the only industry I can think of where most of the employees spend most of their time stating with great self-assurance that they don't know how to do their jobs. "I don't know how to sell this," they complain, frowning as though it's *your* fault. "I don't know how to package this. I don't know what the market is for this book. I don't know how we're going to draw attention to this." In most other occupations, people try to hide their incompetence; only in publishing is it flaunted as though it were the chief qualification for the job.

Out of the thousands of people in an entire huge publishing empire, the only one who cares at all about *your* book is the editor who bought it. He spent the company's money, he made a commitment, and his ongoing reputation—within the firm and within the industry—depends for the moment on your book. When the flacks in publicity fail to tell the difference between the "Today" show and WBAB, Babylon, Long Island, it is the editor who strolls down the hall and chats with the nitwit there. When the art department gives you a jacket that would have looked tired on a Literary Guild selection in 1953, it is the editor who gently suggests that maybe somebody other than the associate art director's roommate might be the best illustrator in this case. When the salesmen scratch their heads and say, "I dunno how to pitch this book. What *is* it, anyway?" it is the editor who explains what the goddam book is, in words clear enough for each salesman to deliver (as though his very own) to book dealers across this mighty land. When the accountant behind the publisher's desk decides four thousand back orders aren't enough to suggest a second printing might be in order, it is the editor who crawls across the Persian rug and says, "Please, Murray, please."

No, the writer cannot do this for himself. Who in the publishing company will listen to a writer? The writer can be expected to be emotional and non-businesslike about this child of his; only the editor can be accepted as a hardheaded professional.

When the editor who bought the book leaves the company before the book is published, the winds blow very cold. In the trade, such a book is called an "orphan," and the word barely suggests the Dickensian—nay, the Hogarthian—horrors that await such a creature. Who shall defend these pitiful pages? Who shall raise this tattered banner from the Out basket? No one.

A new editor is "assigned" to the book, the way homework is assigned to reluctant schoolchildren, and the futility is evident in the word itself. What commitment has this assigned editor in this book? None. How much time and thought will he divert to it from the books *he* chose for the company to publish? Guess.

My gravedigger hasn't been assigned yet. Jack Rosenfarb is to stay on for two more weeks, tidying up his affairs. He assures me he's very excited about the new job that has been offered him by the pay-TV company. May he rot in hell.

And things had been going so well. Jim Davis contributed a drawing of Garfield in a Santa suit that's so charming and cynical at the same time that I've almost lost my hatred for that cat, and Gahan Wilson's drawing of a Christmas tree decorated with any number of tiny hanged men, women and children gave me pause at first, but the more I look at it the more I like it. (I considered asking him to redo it in color, but on second thought that might be dangerous.)

The writers haven't been lax, either. Truman Capote came through with a "Christmas Eve on Death Row" that is touching and strong and a million miles above the staleness of the subject. Arthur C. Clarke sent along a wonderful story about another Christ being born to another species in another galaxy, and John Kenneth Galbraith wrote a reminiscence of a childhood Christmas in Canada that made me smile all day after I read it. Jerzy Kosinski's fantasy about a couple of children living inside a kaleidoscope at the North Pole is maybe a touch *too* cute, but it looks as though he wrote it all himself, and I'm taking it. I don't know quite what to think about Kurt Vonnegut's submarine story, "Captain Nemo's Christmas," and just last Friday I sent it to

Jack Rosenfarb for his opinion. Now, of course, he can take his opinion and shove it.

I have also received several polite turndowns, from (or from the secretaries of) Helen Gurley Brown and Annie Dillard and Gerald Ford and Daniel Patrick Moynihan and Joan Rivers and Isaac Bashevis Singer ("It is not my subject; I'm sorry") and Jonathan Schell and Jamie Wyeth. The "How much?" letter has been received from Ann Beattie, E. L. Doctorow, Richard Nixon, Tom Wolfe, John Simon and Calvin Trillin. A brief typed note from Mickey Spillane said, "You gotta be kiddin'." I wrote him that indeed I was not.

Isaac Asimov has sent me another article, this one on the calendar dating of Christmas. I'd already told him I was taking the aerodynamics-of-the-sleigh piece, so I don't know why he sent another, but he did; anyway, I liked the first one better, so I sent the calendar piece back.

In the middle of all this, Pia Zadora's agent phoned to say his client might be persuaded either (a) to give me a Christmas-theme photo spread, or (b) to contribute a Christmas song she'd written. I said I'd take it up with the staff.

As winter fades, it's becoming harder and harder to think about Christmas. Here it is the end of March, little round pregnant buds protrude from every branch, there's a smell of mud and mildew in the air, spring is on the way, and in the apartment hallway Bryan and

Joshua simultaneously play baseball and soccer. The sight of a pair of boys dressed in Mets caps and first baseman's mitts kicking a soccer ball back and forth is rather *too* heart-warming and Norman Rockwell for somebody who's spending all his waking hours with Christmas anyway, but there they are.

On the other hand, it is nice the way those two boys get along. My Bryan is nine and Ginger's Joshua is ten, and I think maybe they have the best alliance of any of the teams involved in this over-extended family. As is so often the case, their relationship started when they went to bed together. Ginger and I don't have a lot of extra space in this apartment, so whenever my kids stay over Bryan bunks in with Joshua. (Eleven-year-old Jennifer, who does *not* hang out with eight-year-old Gretchen, sleeps on blankets on the floor in Gretchen's room on those occasions.) The boys early discovered a mutual interest in sports and truly rotten television reruns, and have been fast friends ever since. I think I may have to take them to the Mets opener.

But what's going to happen to *The Christmas Book*? With Asimov and Capote and Kosinski and Rooney and Vonnegut and Clarke and Galbraith and Davis and Wilson I've already got name-strength; they *can't* let the book languish now, can they?

Sure they can.

But they've got so much money committed.

Sure they can.

But it's such a great idea.
Sure they can.
But I'm working so *hard*.
Sure they can.
But it's their one best hope for a Christmas book.
Sure they can.
Sure they can.

Monday, March 28th

TOMORROW is the first day of Passover. My new editor told me so today at lunch, several times. In fact, I have come to the conclusion that the purpose of our having lunch had nothing to do with *The Christmas Book*—which was barely mentioned—but that we had gathered at the Tre Mafiosi for sole and chablis so that Ms. Douglas could explain to me what tomorrow, the first day of Passover, meant in the ongoing troubled relationship between herself and her mother, who lives in Fort Lauderdale, in Florida. I feel I know both mother and daughter very well by now; far too well.

Vickie Douglas is a hotshot younger editor, or at least she was until a year or so ago when she crossed the Rubicon of thirty. About five years back, she was the one who plucked out of the slush pile the ex-hooker's diet-and-

pornography book which became known in
the trade as *Fuck Yourself Thin*, but which
Ms. Douglas herself (it is rumored, or claimed)
titled *How a Better Sex Life Can Lead to a
Slimmer You*. With the ex-hooker's national
tour, plus the rather sensational nude exer-
cise photos in the book, it became a mon-
strous bestseller (I choose my words carefully)
and Vickie Douglas immediately left that publisher (and the other not-yet-published books
she'd bought there) for a different publisher
and a better salary. She's been at a number of
houses the last several years, and came to
Craig, Harry & Bourke after leaving Metro-
nome House last fall during a flap that even
got reported gingerly in *Publishers Weekly* (the
Junior Scholastic of this tiny world); it was a
dispute over the title of a famous lesbian golf-
er's autobiography. Ms. Douglas had insisted
it be called *Different Strokes*, while the publisher even more strongly demanded it be
called *The Carol Murphy Story*. (Around the
business, it was generally known as "I Can
Lick Any Woman on the Tour.")

A tall, skinny, dark-blonde woman with a
very large head provided with prominent fa-
cial features, Vickie Douglas is attractive in
an acrylic sort of way, until she starts talking,
and smoking, and knocking her bulging leather
bag over, and dropping ashes in the water
glass, and putting her elbow in the salad, and
jangling her bangles, and staring wide-eyed
like someone who's just received a dirk in the

back in a Hitchcock movie. Her voice is loud and breathy at the same time, and she talks very fast like a mother lying to the truant officer, and her self-involvement is so total I don't understand how she can bear to release herself after she puts a sweater on.

This is the creature who came to bury *The Christmas Book*, not to praise it. "You're doing a fine job," she told me, her wide eyes glazed as she thought about her mother. "It's a very interesting concept," she mumbled, looking around for her roll (it was in her bag). "I don't want to second-guess you, just keep going on as before," she suggested, grapes from her sole *Veronique* rolling across the table.

But intermixed with these platitudes were a few zingers. Frowning at a nearby waiter as though measuring him as a potential stepfather, she brooded, "It's hard to know what the *thrust* of the book is, what its *argument* is." Wiping coffee from her blouse, she mumbled into her chest, "I'm afraid Mr. Wilson isn't very impressed by the *kind* of contributor you've come up with so far. Vonnegut, Galbraith; these are all rather *yesterday*, aren't they?" Staring at the American Express credit card slip, trying to do gratuity mathematics in her head, she mused, "Perhaps the problem is Christmas itself. Perhaps it's just too *ordinary*."

What am I going to do about this woman? I have to do something about this woman, but what? If I kill her, they'll only assign another

editor, and I know what they'd give me next
(assuming I didn't get arrested for murder,
which I surely would). What they would give
me next would be some hundred-year-old, pipe-
smoking fart with a wonderful shock of white
hair and a brain that died in the late nineteenth century, during his second year at Exe-
ter. He would be named something like Ray-
mond Atherton Swifft or Hambleton Cudlipp
the Third, he would not have actually *done*
anything at the firm within living memory,
and once we had become fast friends he would
tell me his one anecdote: the time he got drunk
with John O'Hara, missed his train to Croton,
and had to take the 7:10.

So Victoria Douglas is not the worst possible disaster that could befall *The Christmas
Book;* she's only the second-worst.

I have to do something. There's nothing to
do. But I have to. I have to do something
about this woman.

Monday, April 4th

ANNIE phoned late this afternoon, and said don't worry. But then she said, "That's bull-shit, of course." I have been cursed with an honest agent.

Last Thursday, after brooding about Vickie Douglas for three days, I finally went to see Annie in her office. She listened to my tale of woe, and shook her grizzled head and sighed a grizzled sigh, and said, "Well, Tom, it never comes easy." (We were meeting in the morning.)

"I don't ask it to come easy," I said. "I just ask it to *come*."

"She has a good reputation, Vickie Douglas," Annie said.

"Not with me."

"It was a first impression. Maybe she'll grow on you." But immediately she pointed a gnarled finger at my nose: "If you say, 'Like fungus,' I won't represent you any more."

I had been deciding whether to say "Like fungus." I said, "If she grows on me, I'll have her surgically removed."

"That's not much better. More baroque, but not better."

"Annie, the woman spent two hours talking about her *mother*. The only thing she said about the book was that my celebrities were *yesterday*. The book bores her. I bore her. Everything on God's green Earth bores her except her goddam mother."

"She's had her successes," Annie said doubtfully.

"She doesn't intend *The Christmas Book* to be among them."

"Do you want someone else assigned?"

"Oh, Christ," I said. "Who? If I say I won't work with that bitch, I'll have a reputation around the shop for being difficult and then *nobody* will be on my side. Is Wilson on my side? Is there anybody over there who's *committed* to this book?"

"Well, Wilson did approve it."

"Why doesn't *he* take it over?"

Annie smiled, shaking her head. "Robert Wilson is an executive now," she said. "He doesn't have to work for a living any more."

"My entire life is passing before my eyes," I said. "What does that mean?"

"It means you're self-centered."

"*I'm* self-centered? What does that make Vickie Douglas?"

Annie sighed. "It is a problem," she acknowledged. "I'll go along with you, it is a problem. I'll have a quiet conversation with Wilson, just see what he thinks of things."

"When?"

"Well, this is the worst possible time of year," she said. "Worse than August. Tomorrow's Good Friday, so the Christians won't be around, and the Jews are still contending with Passover."

"The rest of the year," I said bitterly, "they're all atheists."

"Oh, I don't think so," she said. "It's hard to work in publishing without believing there must be a greater Intelligence *somewhere* in the universe."

So it was agreed that Annie would try to talk with Wilson on Monday, being today, and I went away to hang on my own cross over Easter weekend.

Actually, Easter *is* Passover, plus additions, most of them pagan, starting with the name, which comes out of our dim half-forgotten Teutonic past. Just as the northern gods gave us Wednesday (Wodin-his-day; that's why it's spelled funny) and Thursday (Thor, of course) and Friday (either Frey or her sister Freya; don't blame *me*), Easter is derived from a dawn goddess named Eostre or Eostur or Éastre or Ostara or some damn thing, the difference being that maybe she never existed.

A double nonreality, that; a mythical goddess without a myth.

The problem is, the only reference to her is in the Venerable Bede's (672-735) *Ecclesiastical History*, and Bede has taken some knocks recently from people who say he made her up by working back from the Anglo-Saxon name of April, which was *Eostur-monath*.

Maybe so, but I'm with Bede. I mean, otherwise he's pretty reliable, and the name *sounds* right. Anyway, if there ever *was* an Eostur, in the old days, and I mean the *old* days, her feast day was the vernal equinox, when bonfires would be lit in her honor, which makes sense. Also, the sun would start that day with three leaps up from the horizon in a dance of joy, and maidens clothed all in white would appear on mountains and in the clefts of rocks. What these maidens did if you went over and said, "Hi, you come here often?" I do not know, but spring festivals used to be pretty sexy before they reformed and got mixed up with the Christians. The original emphasis on fertility and fecundity is still palely visible in our Easter eggs and Easter rabbits, but the pizzazz is pretty well gone now, and it has merely become the only time of year when you can sell an otherwise sensible woman a lavender coat.

A former Easter custom I wish was still with us was the *Risus Paschalis*, which started in Bavaria in the fifteenth century. The idea was, the priest would tell jokes and funny

stories during Easter Mass, in order to make
the parishioners laugh, the laughter supposed
to be a good gift for the risen Christ. However, the jokes got to be a little sacrilegious
sometimes, so in the eighteenth century the
practice was banned by Pope Maximilian III.

Whenever they hear anybody laughing, boy,
they sure put a stop to it.

Wednesday, April 6th

YESTERDAY I took the boys—my boy Bryan and Ginger's boy Joshua—to the Mets' opener out at Shea. We arrived by subway just before one, the boys as excited as if they were going to heaven instead of Shea Stadium, and we found ourselves in the midst of a large and young and happy crowd. Some people wore large orange buttons that said, in blocky black lettering, NOW THE FUN STARTS! The idea that there hadn't been any fun up till now worked very well into my general mood, but I did my best to fight down my skepticism that things were about to change.

It was perfect opening day weather, sunny and breezy and nippy, which had brought out the Mets' largest opening day crowd since 1968. We had press level seats, out beyond third base, high enough to get a sense of the stadium but low enough to be involved with the game, which the boys certainly were. This was Tom Seaver's return to the Mets after years of exile in Cincinnati, so the occasion began with a standing ovation for Seaver as he walked the length of the right-field foul line to the Mets' dugout.

Much learned discussion took place all around us as to whether the thirty-eight-year-old Seaver still "had it," and how many innings he was likely to pitch; the consensus seemed to be that if he survived four or five, he could be considered to still have it.

The Philadelphia Phillies were the opposition, and their pitcher was Steve Carlton, another thirty-eight-year-old veteran, and from almost the first instant it was clear we were going to be treated to a pitchers' duel. In the first six innings, Carlton permitted only two singles while Seaver allowed three singles and a walk; neither team ever threatened to score.

I spent more and more time watching the outer world beyond the outfield fence, where the big jets sailed slowly by, descending like stately matrons toward LaGuardia Airport, and where the unending traffic of the Van Wyck Expressway hurried along its busy antlike way, elevated above the scruffy neighborhoods. A tower of the Whitestone Bridge could be seen against the pale blue sky, contrasting beautifully with the rich green emptiness of the outfield. "What happens if they *never* score?"

Joshua asked me. "Then the game never ends," I told him.

And through it all, I kept thinking about *The Christmas Book*. Baseball starting, spring in the air, and my mind is filled with Christmas. In the last week I've received several more contributions, and I'm beginning to think the final shape of the book will be a bit odder than I'd originally planned. I did return Diana Trilling's "Christmas In The Gulag," saying we were trying to avoid politics—particularly global politics—in *The Christmas Book*, but William F. Buckley, Jr.'s "Floating Celebration" I just cannot resist. It is a description of a Christmas Eve party on a yacht in the Caribbean, involving himself and his wife Pat and several of their middleweight celebrity friends, and failing a submission from Louis XVI this one has absolutely got to get into the book. What makes it wonderful is that, when Buckley describes the darkies singing carols for the gentry on deck beneath the torrid tropic sun, *he* thinks the subject is the tropic sun.

Isaac Asimov sent me another article, this one on the uses and meanings of gold, frankincense and myrrh in the ancient world. I returned it with thanks; why does he keep sending me things? I've already taken one.

Roddy McDowall sent a nice letter, apologizing for not having written sooner and suggesting a series of photos of famous people opening Christmas presents with their children. He had already accumulated several such

over the years—Elizabeth Taylor, for instance
—so he sent a few contact prints to give me
the idea; lovely luminous black-and-white pictures, very heartwarming in the best possible
way. We don't expect such expressions on famous faces; it could be that the human physi-
ognomy never looks sweeter or more blessed
than when a present is given to a child. I
wrote McDowall how much I liked the idea,
only suggesting en passant that he risked a
certain sameness overall, which I trusted his
genius to be aware of and deal with.

Helmut Newton sent six photos of a naked
woman dressed in various leather belts seated
this way and that way on a department store
Santa's knee. I returned them with a note
saying we'd abandoned the project.

I *like* what Tomi Ungerer sent. I'm not sure
I can use it, but I like it. In a series of drawings, Santa Claus walks through the forest
with his sack over his shoulder, enters a cot-
tage, takes toys and cakes and goodies from
the sack as delighted children gather around
him—coming in from other cottages in the
neighborhood, presumably—and then Santa
grabs up all the children and puts *them* in the
now-empty sack. He walks back through the
forest, sack over shoulder, and into his cave,
where he removes the Santa suit and white
beard and is revealed to be an ogre. Okay!

I have also had occasion to write Andy
Warhol.

Dear Mr. Warhol:

Thank you for the photos of the old round Coca-Cola tray with the smiling Santa Claus face on it, and the Santa Claus hand holding a Coke glass. The outlines you drew around everything in red and green are very thought-provoking, but unfortunately we have already made arrangements with the Coca-Cola Bottling Company, Atlanta, Georgia, to print a representation of the same tray in The Christmas Book. *Not with your additions, of course, but perhaps the simple original will work best within our context.*

What I did, when I got the Warhol package, was immediately phone the Coca-Cola company, and spoke to a PR woman there, and once she understood this was a legitimate middle-class operation with a respectable publishing company behind it she agreed I could use the tray photo for free. Those who wish doodles on the picture can mark up their own copies in the privacy of their homes.

In the meantime, despite Annie's assurances, the greater shadow still looms over the book and me and all living things: Vickie Douglas continues to be my editor. Annie's discussion with Wilson changed nothing. Day after day I am involving myself with this book—not only in correspondence with potential contributors, but also in library research for oldies and goodies, and in poring at home over endless anthologies and collections—and all the time, from the far distance, I can hear the slow beat of that muffled drum. "Vick-ie Doug-las," the drum says, steady and deadly. "Vick-ie Doug-las. Vick-ie Doug-las."

I couldn't even forget it yesterday during the ball game. At the top of the seventh Seaver, suffering a strained leg muscle, was replaced by a rookie named Doug Sisk, who maintained the steady pace, retiring the side without trouble. Unable to fight it any more, following that third out I got to my feet. As the Phillies trotted back onto the field, Carlton still leading them, and Dave Kingman (who had already struck out three times in this game) coming up to bat, I excused myself to the boys and walked back around the press level to the Diamond Club bar, where I found a phone booth and called Craig, Harry & Bourke and, after some small delay, spoke with my *bête noire* in more or less person. She remembered me almost right away, and I said, "Vickie, I'm worried."

"Worried? About what?"

"About *us*," I said. "You and me. Maybe I was distracted or something last week, but I just don't feel we had that real meeting of minds we should—"

"Oh, you didn't?" She sounded mildly surprised. "Well, of course, we were just getting to know one another, that sort of thing always takes . . ." She faded away, apparently torn between ending the sentence falsely (". . .

time.") or truthfully (". . . forever."). Outside,
the crowd roared.

"Vickie," I said loudly, in case she was falling asleep, "I'm not one of your prima don-
nas, one of those people who can't take advice
or help. I *believe* in a strong relationship between author and editor. This is a very important project for me, Vickie, and I—"

"Well, sure it is."

"And I want us to work on it together. I
want your input, I want you to feel this is
your book as much as it is mine."

"Oh, that's sweet," she said. "But honestly,
Tom, *I* think an editor who stomps all over a
book, leaves his own footprints everywhere,
isn't doing *anybody* any favors. This is your—"

"*Our,* Vickie. Mine in concept, mine for the
most part in execution, but yours in translating
that concept and work.into a marketable, sell-
able package, something that Craig, Harry—"

"Oh, Tom," she said, "you should never let
commercial consid—"

"I just want the best book possible," I said
quickly, desperately. When your editor tells
you not to let commercial considerations stand
in your way, you *know* you're doomed. "And,"
I scrambled on, "with you there to be sure I
don't go astray, I can—"

"I have every confidence in you, Tom," the
bitch said, while far away the damn crowd
roared again for some reason.

We went on like that, flinging the responsibility like a baseball at one another, putting

ever-increasing spin on it, neither of us getting anywhere. I was reminded of the old movie cartoons where Daffy Duck and Yosemite Sam would throw the smoking bomb back and forth until it finally exploded, and in every case it blew up while Yosemite Sam was holding it. I have considered our personalities and our relationship, and I have come to the reluctant conclusion that Vickie Douglas is Daffy Duck.

The end result of the phone call was that we made another lunch date, during which we can get to know and hate one another even better. Next Tuesday it is, the twelfth. Another lunch. Now the fun starts.

Another result of the phone call was that I missed the only action of the afternoon. Dave Kingman, whom I'd been relying on to strike out again, started the inning with a single into left field, followed by a George Foster single to right, moving Kingman to second. Hubie Brooks was next, and his sacrifice bunt was so perfect it wasn't even a sacrifice; he beat the throw to first, loading the bases. Then came Mike Howard, who bounced another single into left, scoring Kingman. Brian Giles, up next, belted a long one into right field that Pete Rose caught for the out, but Foster scored after the catch, making it two to zip with men on first and second, and only one out.

And that's when I returned from my phone call, to find the boys careening around in our area like Mexican jumping beans. They both simultaneously tried to tell me all the terrific

stuff I'd missed, while I sat there and listened
and thought about Vickie Douglas and watched
Steve Carlton get things back under control,
putting out the next two men at bat and returning the game to its pitchers' duel, which
it remained until the end. So the Mets won
their opener, two to nothing, making nine seasons in a row in which they've won the opening game, tying the record (1937–45) of the
St. Louis Browns, and I am still flailing away
with *The Christmas Book*.

I do not want to hear any more about Vickie
Douglas's *mother*.

~~~~~~~~~~~~~~~~~

Sunday, April 10th

ANOTHER expense. Ginger and I just came
back from Fire Island, where we looked at
rental houses. The train from Penn Station
got us to Bay Shore in time for the 1:00 ferry
over to Fair Harbor on Fire Island, where we
had about an hour and a half to look at houses
and to walk in the thin sunlight on the cold
tan beach, hand in hand, smiling foolishly,
before taking the 3:10 ferry off again. It was
nice to be out there, nice to see the early
spring flowers and smell the salt air with its
promise of summer, nice to stop thinking about
Christmas (and that awful woman!) for just a
little while.

Summer house rentals are outrageous; they
always have been, and they get worse every
year. We saw at once that we wouldn't be
able to afford August, the more expensive

month, so we resigned ourselves to the second-class existence of being July renters. (And even that can only be afforded if Vickie Douglas and her superiors at Craig, Harry & Bourke agree on June first that five of my contributors are sufficiently *today* and famous to activate the next stage of the contract. With Vonnegut and Galbraith already having been dismissed, who knows *what* names would impress that awful woman?)

One of the complications in our rental search is that we need a very large house, since we will have all four kids with us—Ginger's two and my two—and to be able to afford the full month of July we have to give accommodation to Mary for two weeks within it.

Talk about being between a rock and a hard place! When Mary first suggested this insane idea, I quite naturally said no, no, a thousand times no and assumed that was the end of it. But it was not. The discussion took place in Mary's kitchen, over cups of coffee, a couple of Sundays ago, after I brought the kids back from their weekend romp with Papa. Jennifer and Bryan had gone away to the living room to watch *60 Minutes*, leaving me at Mary's mercy, and we spent a while looking at contact prints of a series of pictures she'd done for some goody-goody youth magazine. They showed a young girl (Jennifer) making a birdhouse; sawing, nailing, painting, etc. In every photo, Jennifer wore the identical solemn and rigid expression, which seemed to me wrong.

I said, "She doesn't look like she's making a birdhouse, she looks like she's posing for pictures."

"It's very hard to break through that self-consciousness." Mary sighed, tapping a fingernail on perhaps the worst of the batch: Jennifer, solemn, looked unemotionally at a hammer she held perched atop a nail partway stuck into a board. "I don't want to send these in if they're not right," Mary said. "It's a new market for me, I don't want to screw it up."

I could only agree with that sentiment. Mary's occasional photography sales, and her more frequent research jobs, were in truth a mere drop in the bucket of my financial responsibilities, but every drop helps. I said, "Why not have Jennifer build a birdhouse, and take pictures while she's doing it?"

Smiling ruefully, Mary said, "Well, she's not very good at it, is the problem. I hate to say such a thing, but she hammers like a girl."

There are these moments in life, when reality gets in the way of our best intentions. "Hmm," I said.

"And the pictures come out confused anyway," she went on. "I really *have* to do posed shots, because the whole point is to show other kids how it's done."

"And inspire them," I suggested, "with pictures of a girl who can."

"Yes." She frowned at the prints. "Maybe if

she held the hammer up in the air, it would be better."

"If she could manage to look at the nail as though she wanted to hit it," I said, "that might also help."

"We'd better shoot another series," she decided, pushed the contact pages to one side, and looked at me with deceptive calmness as she said, "Do you know what you're going to do this summer?"

"We'll try to rent a house for a month out on Fire Island," I said. "Take all the kids out there."

"Which month?"

"I don't know yet. Depends on rental prices, what we can find. Ginger can shuffle her vacation schedule around, so we have some flexibility."

"I'll want to know pretty soon," she said, "so I can make arrangements for the other month and tell you how much money I'll need."

I looked at her. "Money?"

"Well, *I'll* have to take the children somewhere, too."

Two months of summer rental? "I can't afford that, Mary," I said. (Last year, they'd stayed a month up in Greene County with another separated mommy and her kids, old friends of ours.)

She smiled, shaking her head at me; clearly, I just didn't understand the situation. "We're your family, Tom," she said. "You don't say you can't afford your family."

"I do say it. Besides, I'll be taking Jennifer and Bryan for a month."

"Vacation is two months."

"Mary, that's all I can handle."

"You expect me, Tom, to stay in the city the entire summer?"

Oh, hell. "Mary," I said, "what am I supposed to *do*?"

"You know what you're supposed to do."

Well, we wrangled for a while, and then she said, "Why not take a place for the whole season? Then you and Ginger could have it half the time, and the children and I could have it the rest."

"I *told* you, I can't afford it. I can barely afford the one month."

"Then we'll divide *that* in half," she said. "Two weeks for you and two weeks for me."

"Oh, no. Oh, no, you don't."

"I tell you what, Tom," she said, with that infuriating smile. "I'll let you stay out there during my two weeks if you want. And Ginger, of course, and the children."

"No," I said. "No, no, a thousand times no."

She shrugged, unruffled. "Well, you'll have to think of something," she said.

So I spent time thinking about her ideas. She *knew* I wouldn't be able to just walk away from my goddam responsibility—why, oh, *why* won't she get a fella?—so it came down to one of two choices: Either I come up with the money for Mary to take her own month in the sun (which I very grudgingly acknowledge she should get, if I'm getting such a month), or Ginger and I share two weeks of our summer vacation with her.

If I had all the money in the world, I wouldn't have any problems, right? Or, at least not *these* problems. I tossed and turned and wriggled and squirmed on the end of that harpoon for several days before first broaching the subject to Ginger, who stared at me as though I had just dyed my hair green. She said, "Are you *crazy*?"

"I can't *afford* to give her a month, Ginger. And it's only two weeks."

"Only!"

"Think of her as a kind of built-in baby-sitter," I said. "Freeing us for—"

"A mother's helper." Ginger's voice dripped with scorn.

"In a way," I said.

"No," Ginger said. "No, no, a thousand times no."

"That's what I said when Mary first suggested it."

"Oh, that bitch!" Ginger said. "That devious conniving bitch!"

"Wait a minute, wait a minute. What's so devious? Everything's right out on the surface. Ginger, you can't deny the woman deserves a—"

"Deserves! What about *me*?"

"We're having a *month*!" I yelled, getting mad. "She's getting two lousy weeks!"

"And they will be lousy, you can bet on that!"

"Not for us, Ginger," I said. "I promise. We can live our own life, have nothing to do with Mary at all."

"Living in the same house."

"We'll find the right house," I said. "Something with a separate entrance or something. Besides, think of it this way. If Mary *sees* us together for a couple of weeks, sees how wonderfully we get along together—"

"Hah."

"So we'll *get* along, dammit! Do you have to be so goddam *selfish* all the time? Can't you see—"

"Selfish! Am *I* forcing myself onto somebody else's—"

It went on like that for a while, although louder. Ginger threw a book and an ashtray and a copy of *New York* magazine, but not at me. Then she abruptly stormed out of the room, slammed the bedroom door behind her, and wouldn't speak to me for two days; so that's how I knew I'd won the fight.

A new variant on the Pyrrhic victory. After arguments and rages and trouble with *two* women, I have at last achieved a goal I don't want. Don't ask me how such things happen, they just do. I am not looking forward to sharing a house with Ginger and Mary for two minutes, let alone two weeks, but there it is.

After the real-estate lady showed us several formica-and-linoleum chalets—places designed so they can be hosed down after the filthy renters depart—we finally found on Laurel Walk a place peculiarly suited to our peculiar needs. An older house, clapboard outside and homosote within, it has two bedrooms and a bath downstairs and one bedroom with its own tiny bath as a later addition upstairs. Out back, across the wooden deck, is a small guest-house, complete with its own bath. *That's* where we put Mary, and the kids go in the downstairs bedrooms, and Ginger and I will be able to retire to peace and privacy all alone upstairs. My hand trembled slightly as I signed the deposit check, but within the range of options open to me I think I made the right decision.

So why do I feel so nervous?

Tuesday, April 12th

WELL. Vickie Douglas. Well. This will bear some thinking about.

Normally I drink very lightly during a business lunch—nothing stronger than wine, and that paced carefully through the meal—but I was so troubled by the very thought of the woman, not to mention her actual presence at table with me, that when the waiter asked us if we'd like to start with something from the bar, I immediately said, "Bourbon and soda."

(When did waiters start saying, "Would you like to start with something from the bar?" It seems to me that up till a few years ago waiters used to say, "Would you care for a drink before lunch?" Is this some sort of dainty-pinky euphemism, avoiding the dread word *drink*? One of these days, I am going to answer a waiter, "Yes. I would like a barstool from the bar. You can send it to this address.")

But not this time. This time I asked for bourbon, and Vickie said, "That sounds good. The same for me." After the waiter retired, she said, "I could use a drink. I took the long weekend in Florida, and my mother—"

"I noticed the tan," I said.

"I had to get out of the house. My mother . . ."

And so on.

We received our drinks and I slurped mine in a kind of heavy paralyzed frenzy, while Vickie slogged through a rerun of the argument she and her mother had most recently had on the subject of why Vickie still wasn't married. "I tell her it's *my choice*, it's nothing to do with her, she's so unenlightened, she wants me to be an earthmother like her, nothing but soup and cabbage and babies, no *thought* of the great world outside her kitchen, the entire women's revolution might never have happened, to hear her you could . . ."

Oh, God; oh, God; oh, God.

The waiter asked if we were ready to order. "I haven't even *looked* at the menu," Vickie said. "Give us a minute. And bring me another drink. Tom?"

"Oh, definitely," I said.

We looked at the menu. I will *not* have sole *Veronique*, I told myself. I didn't want sweetbreads, I didn't want the veal Marsala, I don't believe human beings should eat pork chops at lunchtime, and it's possible I hate frittata.

When the waiter returned with our fresh drinks and his order pad, I said, "I'll have the sole *Veronique*."

"Sweetbreads," Vickie said, which was her most interesting statement to date. Then the waiter went away and Vickie's mother re-entered, like Banquo, and joined us at the table.

The waiter brought salads, and Vickie said, "I forgot to order wine. How about this Pouilly-Fumé?"

"Of course, Madame."

"And another round."

"Certainly."

It was partway through that third drink that I put the glass down beside my untasted salad and said, "Vickie. Shut. Up."

She blinked at me. Her eyes became more than usually owlish. "Tom?"

"Vickie," I said, "I have had enough. I don't give a royal fuck about your mother. I figure she's probably just another self-centered big-mouth like you, and she deserves you just as much as you deserve her. But *I* don't deserve either of you."

I have never in my life seen as astonished an expression as was then on Vickie's face. The waiter arrived at that moment, bearing food, and as he reached to place her oval plate of sweetbreads before her, Vickie said, "Why, you utter horse's ass."

The waiter jerked slightly. Butter sauce

slopped. Frowning intently, he placed the plate to cover the stain.

Meanwhile, I was going through some sort of death agony, I was becoming unborn. My stomach had turned into a gnarled old rain forest during an electrical storm, my cheekbones had reached a thousand degrees Fahrenheit and were beginning to melt, and hot smelly suety perspiration was breaking out all over my head and body. "Oh, my God," I said. "Vickie, I'm terribly sorry."

"Have you lost your *mind*?"

"Yes," I said. The waiter was coming around the table with my sole *Veronique*. "Listen, Vickie," I said. "My girlfriend is jealous of my wife."

Why I started my explanation/apology at that particular point in my tale of woe I don't know, but the waiter's reaction was to take one deliberate pace backward, still holding my plate, and give me a severe look, as though he suspected me of trying deliberately to break his concentration. "Oh, put it down," I snapped at him—I was snapping in many ways, and in many directions—and he did, and then he went away, and I opened my mouth and unburdened myself to the cold-eyed, hot-eyed Vickie.

I told her everything. My financial problems, my problems with Mary's refusal to get a fella, the resulting problems with Ginger so that, while our sex life was still terrific, the time spent out of bed was becoming increasingly grim. I told her what *The Christmas Book* meant in all this, and I told her my fears about what would happen when I lost my editor, and I told her she had done nothing to alleviate those fears and everything to increase them.

During this monologue—Vickie remained silent, unblinking eyes fixed on me—we switched from bourbon to wine and did a very, very small amount of eating; maybe one organ for her and one grape for me. And when at last I ran out of things to say, and sputtered brokenly into a silence dotted with a few last apologies, there was practically no wine left, I had no appetite for food, and Vickie let at least a minute of dead air go by before saying, calmly but coldly, "I do not talk about my mother all the time."

"You do," I said.

"You're paranoid," she said. "It's your paranoia. I do not talk about my mother all the time."

"You do, you do, you do." Leaning forward over my plate, I said, "Vickie, do you think I have nervous breakdowns during lunch *every* day?"

She studied me, large dark inscrutable eyes. Would she never blink again?

Yes; a long slow blink. She sighed, and looked away at last across the room. "Maybe I do," she said.

"I'm sorry, Vickie," I said. "I know you're having trouble with her, I don't mean to be heartless about this, I—"

"But there's no reason for you to give a shit about my mother," she said, nodding, not looking at me. "I know."

"I wouldn't phrase it quite like that," I said.

"You already did."

"Oh. Sorry."

Another sigh. But then she frowned, and did look back at me. She said, "But that has nothing to do with *us*, with your book."

"You don't like my book."

"That's absurd," she said.

I said, "You told me Christmas was too ordinary to think about."

"I never did!"

"Two weeks ago, at lunch, that table over there. You said Kurt Vonnegut and John Kenneth Galbraith were yesterday."

"I did? What did I mean?" Now she was blinking a *lot*.

"I think you meant you were bored," I said.

"It's my mother," she said, nodding owlishly. "I think about her, and *everything* looks rotten. Do you know, last Saturday in Fort Lauderdale, my mother had the ner—"

"Vickie," I said. "*Please*."

"Oh, shit," she said. "I do talk about her all the time." She reached out and knocked over her wine glass. "Shit again," she said. "You want coffee?"

"No," I said.

"You want another drink?"

"Yes, but I better not. I'm feeling what I already had."

"So am I. Let's get out of here." With her other forearm resting in the salad, she waved exuberantly for the waiter.

While she was going through the credit card routine, she said, "I don't blame you, Tom. When I get back to the office I'll talk to Wilson, he can assign you another editor."

"Find me an orphan," I suggested, trying for levity.

"Mm," she said, nodding morosely. "What a lovely sound that word has."

We bought our coats back from the checkroom and went out to Park Avenue, where the cool damp spring air made us both totter; I was feeling my drinks more and more. Pawing in her huge leather bag for some reason, weaving back and forth on the sidewalk, Vickie said, "Shit. *I'm* not going back to the office. I'm going home and feel sorry for myself."

"Me, too."

"I'll talk to Wilson tomorrow."

"Good. No hard feelings?"

"Since when, you prick?" She glared at me, but then something in my expression made her laugh. She said, "Of course there's hard feelings, but we're grown-ups, we'll get over it."

"My wife is to me what your mother is to you," I said.

"I will not stand here while you get even with me by talking about your *wife*," she said. "I am going to get a cab." She lunged toward the curb.

I lunged after her, afraid she would either fall or get run over, and it would be my fault. I said, "Wait a minute. Where do you live?"

"West 86th."

There was an empty cab a block away; I semaphored it. "I'm on 70th," I said. "We can share, if it's okay with you."

"Sure. I'm liberal."

We got in the cab and I told the driver, "Two stops." Then, because I was feeling guilty and chivalrous, I said, "West 86th Street first," even though my place would have been closer.

The cabby took us up Park, and we sat back on the lumpy seat with the stingy legroom, and I said, "I'm sorry, Vickie, I really am."

"Maybe I should go back into analysis," she said.

"You used to?"

"Two and a half years. Money I could have spent on clothing, thrown away trying to become a good daughter." She glared at me, speaking through clenched teeth. "Not once did that sonofabitch tell me, to be a good daughter you have to have a good mother!"

"Well, you found out," I said.

"It doesn't help," she said, and glared out the window instead.

Being in close contact with a crazy person becomes physically painful. Your shoulders bunch up as you wait for what's going to happen next. I sat there, warm in my coat, uncomfortable, waiting for this sequence to

be over, and thought about my next editor.
Hambleton Cudlipp the Third.

On our way through the park she started to
cry, little smeerpy sounds and tiny acid tears
squeezing out of her eyes. Head averted, she
poked and pawed through all the crap and
horseshit in her bag. I said, "You're crying!"

"I am not," she gritted, low and intense.
She wouldn't look at me; her head was practically in her leather bag now, as she kept searching for a tissue or a handkerchief. "Nothing
on Earth makes me madder than to cry in
public," she muttered, grinding her teeth.
"*Therefore* I am not crying *now*."

"Okay," I said.

At her apartment house, I paid and got out
with her. "I'll walk down Columbus," I said.
"I want to be sure you're all right."

"I'm fine," she said, staggering on the sidewalk. She wasn't crying any more, but her
face was blotchy. "I'm peachy. *Destroyed* at
fucking lunch with a writer. Home a basket
case. Go away, you sonofabitch."

"Vickie," I said, "I'm not the psychiatrist.
I'm not even your mother. Will you be okay?"

"No," she said. She stared at me. "Which
one of us is the bastard? Am I wrong, or are
you wrong?"

"I think we're both right," I said. "It's just
unfortunate that—"

"Fucking platitudes."

"You're right," I said. "The truth is, I think
you're a self-centered bitch, and I'm in just as

much trouble as I was before, and I don't know if the next asshole's gonna be even worse or not."

"Oh, I got a guy for you," she said, with a nasty little grin. "He edits all our war books."

"What a shit you are," I said, but I had to laugh when I said it.

"Come on up, I'll buy ya a drink," she said.

"It's the least you can do," I told her.

She had a tiny high-floor apartment in a once-graceful large old building in which the dignified big apartments were long ago chopped into these ant-runs. Books, posters, stereo equipment, and here and there a narrow place to sit. The kitchen was too small for two people; I stood in the doorway while she failed to find bourbon, and we agreed to switch to vodka and grapefruit juice. "It's a food," she said. "We won't get drunk."

"Very important," I agreed.

She made the two drinks and turned toward the doorway with one in each hand. I reached out and cupped my hand around the back of her head and drew her close and kissed her lips.

I was appalled at myself while I was doing it. I'm merely astonished now, but I may go on being astonished about that bit of autobiography the rest of my life. I'm not on the prowl for yet another woman, God knows, and I don't go around throwing heavy-handed passes just because an opportunity appears. I didn't even *like* Vickie Douglas. And yet I kissed her.

It wasn't a long kiss. Neither of us opened our mouths. At the end, I released her, and she stepped back and stared at me. "Now, why in hell," she said, "did you do *that*?"

"I don't know," I said truthfully, knowing I'd found the one way to make an impossible situation worse. "I just did it. How many drinks are you going to throw in my face?"

"I'm not sure." She stood there, thinking, holding the glasses. She licked her upper lip, as though the taste would suggest an attitude. "Maybe," she said thoughtfully, "maybe what we ought to do is just fuck."

Oh, my gosh. Mary, Ginger . . . I can't handle this, I thought, I've got to get out of here, undo this somehow. But it was too late. With horror I watched her put the glasses down on the counter and turn toward me with an expression of expectant curiosity.

I just couldn't be that rude.

The Christmas Book, I told myself. Do it for *The Christmas Book*.

When I left there at quarter to five we'd agreed she would stay on as my editor. We'll be having another editorial meeting on Thursday.

Thursday, April 28th

I own a tiger. Or maybe the tiger owns me. Whichever it is, I'm sure *riding* the tiger.

Vickie and I have been burning bright for two and a half weeks now, and I must admit my guilt and terror are both at last receding, though by no means am I easy in my mind. How long can this possibly continue without Ginger suspecting? I am being very careful not to bring any new ideas home, but how can I be sure Ginger—whose intuitive and paranoiac antennae are wonderfully fine-honed—won't notice some bedtime change in me? Also, I'm losing weight.

On the professional side, what has happened is all to the good. Vickie has now become a tiger in the office as well, pushing *The Christmas Book* as though the Mafia had ordered her to. She's agitating with the art and pro-

131

duction departments to give us something spectacular for the dust jacket and the general package, she's hustling the legal department and the rights department for all the necessary papers on both original material and reprints, and although it's really too early to do so she's talking it up in sales meetings, assuring everyone that Craig, Harry & Bourke will have a great year just because of *The Christmas Book* no matter what happens to the rest of the list.

She is also trying to get the company to move right away to the next phase of our step deal, confirming their intent to publish, even though they don't contractually have to come up with the next chunk of money until June first. But she's arguing that I've already got many more than five famous names (none of my contributors are *yesterday* any more), and she points out passionately but reasonably that the sooner Craig makes that final commitment to go ahead with the book, the sooner they can start a major sales and promotion campaign.

As for the book itself, it continues to shape up, though in strange ways. For instance, I now have Norman Mailer's submission, and by God if it isn't "Christmas on Death Row"! It's not at all the same as Capote's, it's equally terrific, and I don't know what the hell to do with it. If Vickie and I ever have a quiet moment together, I'll ask her advice; she is my editor, after all.

Up till now, the religious side of Christmas—
and it does have a religious side, mustn't forget that—had been pretty absent from the
new contributions, and I'd been filling it in
mostly from older material, but that is at last
changing. Joyce Carol Oates's piece, an interior monologue by the Virgin Mary in the
manger, is all rather murky, as though it were
menopause rather than childbirth she'd just
gone through, but her reflections on the female role in the religious impulse, however
ornately expressed, are pretty good.

Somehow I never really expected to hear from
Richard Nixon, not even after I got his how-
much letter, but here by God is a neatly-typed
piece about Nixon meeting with Khrushchev
on Christmas Eve and the two of them dis-
cussing Christianity. Nixon portrays himself as a kind of super insurance salesman, all
honest concern and noble patter, and Khrushchev as gruff but innately honest, with talk
of Christmas and religion forcing him into
acknowledgment of his peasant past. Nixon
himself seems to have no past, which may be
what makes him our representative American.

Someone else I thought I'd heard the last of
was Mario Puzo, after that snotty letter his
person sent me, but just the other day I got
his contribution, and it's wonderful. He tells
about going to midnight Mass with his family
as a little kid, and the flavors of Roman Ca-
tholicism, of America and of his family's Italian

heritage are blended together into a rich and heartening stew.

On the visual side, LeRoy Nieman's three Wise Men on a hilltop with a whole *hell* of a lot of bloodshot sky behind them and several odd rough-hewn patches of white or blue paint placed at random in irrelevant spots is not exactly *terrible*. I am taking it because (a) he's a name, and (b) it might get the book some ink in *Playboy*. I console myself with the thought that if I'd been putting this book together just a few years ago I would have had to make room for Peter Max.

Or would he have said no? Edward Albee has, and so have Steven Spielberg, Henry Kissinger, Sam Shepard and Jasper Johns. I'd been thinking of putting together a followup letter for those people I haven't heard from at all—which is only thirty out of seventy-five, a damn good response—but now I think I don't need it; I'm getting some heavy hitters here.

I have returned Isaac Asimov's article about Mrs. Claus's functions up there in Santa Claus's workshop at the North Pole. I have also returned Mr. Asimov's piece about the etymology of the name Santa Claus, with all the other things Saint Nicholas is called around the world. I think the man is trying to drive me crazy.

Sunday, May 8th

MOTHER'S DAY!!!!!

I am in here hiding from everybody. As the sun moves to the horizon and our ship sinks slowly in the west, we bid farewell to the friendly huts and rude natives of . . . of home, I guess.

This weekend began to unravel on Friday, when I stayed so long at Vickie's place that I had to tear straight home by cab in order to be here by a plausible hour—the story was that I had met with my editor in her *office*, naturally, not in her bed, and there's a limit to how late I can return from somebody's office—and Ginger was already home from *her* office when I got there. She kissed me hello, then wrinkled up her nose and said, "What's that smell?"

Oh, my God. What musk, what rutting scent

of lust, what steamy reminder of passion still lurked on my flesh? Trying desperately not to look guilty, I said, "Smell? What smell?"

She sniffed. She frowned. She sniffed again. She gave me a *very* skeptical look. "Soap," she said.

"Oh!" My mind fishtailed wildly. I smelled my hands, which were trembling. "It must be that damn stuff in the men's room," I said. "You know, that pink liquid they give you? I pressed on the thing, and it squirted all over the place. You can still smell it, huh?"

"Yes," she said. Her eyes were very slightly narrowed, but frown lines of indecision were visible on her brow.

"I'll go wash it off," I said, and made it away from those scanning eyes as rapidly (but casually) as I could.

Ginger said no more about it, though during dinner she did say, "We ought to invite this new editor of yours to dinner sometime. I really ought to meet her."

Everything in life happens because something else happened before it. In this case, soap had led directly to a dinner invitation. Pretending I didn't see the connection, I said, "That's a good idea. She's very important to us, we ought to cultivate her." Ooh; was that too ambiguous?

Maybe not. Ginger nodded, eyes completely unnarrowed, and said, "Is she married?"

"I don't think so."

"Boyfriend, then. Or girlfriend?"

"Gee," I said. "I have no idea."

"Who should we have for a third couple?"

We chatted about that. I wondered if Ginger's mind was running as rapidly behind her idle chatter as mine was behind mine. After a while, Gretchen—we eat with the children—changed the subject (my heart warmed to her) by saying, "I did a painting for Jennifer's birthday."

The next day—yesterday, now—was to be (has now been) Jennifer's twelfth birthday. Gretchen continues to be an inextinguishable visual artist, though her Christmas drawings for my book have at last dribbled away to nothing. (I was thinking for a while of sending her to Isaac Asimov.) It was now my job to ask to see this painting and to be supportive, so I did and was.

It was pretty good, actually, within its limitations. Jennifer's birthday being in May, and that being traditionally and famously the month of flowers, Gretchen had done, on a twelve-by-sixteen sketchpad sheet, a watercolor of a field *ablaze* with flowers. From across the room it looks almost like a later Jackson Pollock drip painting, but up close it is all these *flowers*, lovingly copied from books and magazines and calendars, crowded in great colorful profusion over the entire sheet of paper.

I did *not* say it looked like a January-sale pillowcase from Macy's. I told Gretchen it was beautiful, and that I was sure Jennifer would love it, and we all admired it for a while. I was very, very good, and much later in bed Ginger said, "Gretchen knows you don't like her."

I said, naturally, "What?"

"If you could see the way you *look* when you talk to her."

"That's ridiculous. I told her how great the picture was."

"She could tell what you really thought. We *all* could tell. Gretchen *happens* to be my daughter, you know."

"I'm well aware of that."

"And what's *that* tone of voice supposed to mean?"

"Ginger, I didn't come to bed to fight."

Nevertheless, we fought. I have nothing against Gretchen, but somehow that isn't enough for Ginger. I'm not sure, on the subject of Gretchen, what *would* be enough for Ginger. The argument didn't get anywhere simply because there was nowhere for it to go, but on the other hand it showed no sign of ending, so after a while I got up and sat in the living room and sulked. Ginger didn't follow me, either to make up or continue the fight, and when I went back to the bedroom—either to make up or continue the fight—she was asleep, so that was that.

Then came yesterday, Jennifer's birthday. I know as well as Ginger, as well as anybody, that this heavy nuclear family schtick of Mary's is all a plot to get me back—even though it's exactly the same way she acted when we were together, which helped to send me away in the first place—but I've nevertheless really got to be *present* for my daughter's birthday, whether it works in with my ex-wife's scheming or not. But try to use logic in these things; go ahead.

It was hard to tell whether Ginger's morning coolness was a carryover from the bedtime argument or a statement of attitude about the current day's program; whichever it was, I pretended to see nothing wrong, got through the morning with no harsh words from anybody, and at eleven-thirty Joshua and Gretchen and I took the subway downtown for Jennifer's birthday lunch.

Complicated families lead to complicated arrangements. Ginger's kids and I arrived at noon for a buffet party/lunch to which about a dozen of Jennifer's female friends had also been invited. At two that crowd left, and Mary and I had the four kids—ours and Ginger's—for an hour, during which the boys went off to Bryan's room to play and Mary discussed Gretchen's painting with her in a very good and supportive way, asking the names of individual flowers, complimenting the kid on so accurately getting the comparative sizes of all the different ones, and telling her she should title the picture "Heavenly Field," because it's so much better than real-world fields. Flowers from different parts of the world and flowers that bloom at different seasons all blossom together in this picture: "Like a chorus of flower angels," Mary said at one point. She didn't overpraise, but she made her interest so clear that the birthday girl, Jennifer, who had at first been rather obviously indifferent to the present, eventually said she would put it on the wall in her room. Gretchen, naturally, basked in all this attention, grinning from ear to ear and swinging her feet back and forth under her chair, as though it were *her* birthday.

At three Lance arrived to take his two away for the rest of the weekend, and Mary and Jennifer and Bryan and I settled around the kitchen table to play the boardgame version of Uno—one of my presents to the birthday girl—until five-thirty, when I left to walk down to the Village, meeting Ginger in front of the Waverly, where we saw the six o'clock showing of the movie, followed by dinner in a very pleasant neighborhood restaurant called the Paris Commune, over on Bleecker Street. I frequently feel I'm in a commune myself, with this olio of parents and children all swimming around in the same stew, but Ginger and I were out of the stew for once last night, and it was one of the best evenings in memory: no edginess, no complication, no defensiveness, no guilt.

Then came today. Goddam *Mother's* Day! A fake, a palpable fake, nothing real in it at all. Nothing even sentimental, if you look at it with a cold clear eye. It's the cynical invention of greeting card manufacturers and candy-makers, that's all it is, a lot of Republican bastards making a dollar off everybody's guilt trips.

Mother's Day was started in 1907, an early example of economic pump-priming, one of the desperate ploys to push consumer spending during the Panic of that year (which was the same year, by the way, that immigration into this country was first legally restricted—so much for sentiment). In that same year, proving it was really the moment to work motherhood for all the profit it contained, Maxim Gorky published his proletarian novel, titled with modest simplicity *Mother*, in which a mother is tricked by the Czar's secret police into betraying her son, a revolutionary, during the failed 1905 rebellion in Russia. How's that for shamelessness? (Not on the part of the secret police; on the part of the writer.)

Mother's Day. They oughta put back the other two syllables.

There was no way, of course, that Mary could let Mother's Day go by without making use of it in this indefatigable campaign of hers; the kids *required* my presence to help them honor their origin. Sure they did.

As for Ginger, my being dragged away to Mary's place two days in a row would have made her testy all by itself; the fact that her own kids were away with Lance and there was nobody around to honor *her* as a mother put her right completely round the bend. Oh, I can't tell you.

In fact, I won't tell you. I behaved at least as badly as anybody else. I am in here hiding from everybody, and in my considered opinion mothers shouldn't be honored, they should be shot on sight.

Thursday, May 19th

LANCE is living in my office.

I type that, and even I can't believe it, but there it is. Lance is living in my office, just down the hall from here. The one place I had in the world where I could close out everybody and everything and just breathe free for a little while, and now Lance is living in it, and I've set up my typewriter on this folding table here in the bedroom.

I don't blame the poor bastard; *he* doesn't want this any more than I do or Ginger does. It just happened, that's all.

What has occurred here, Helena threw him out. Lance swears he wasn't involved in any hanky-panky with any other woman, that it wasn't actually *him* at all, that what Helena had had enough of suddenly was New York City. And perhaps another thing Helena had

had enough of was Helena, because her abrupt
decision (Lance says it was abrupt, anyway)
was to change *everything*. She took her kids
out of school, she told Lance the relationship
was through, she sublet the apartment, and
she went to Santa Fe.

Santa Fe!

Is this the act of a rational woman? Santa Fe,
from East 93rd Street?

Whatever the situation, the point is that
Lance lived with Helena in Helena's apartment (just as I am living with Ginger in Ginger's apartment), so when Santa Fe called to
Helena with its siren call, Lance had to leave.
(Although Helena was subletting her apartment, she would not sublet it to Lance because she was ending their relationship.)

Robert Frost said it: Home is the place
where, when you have to go there, they have
to take you in. Apparently that's still true,
even under such weird conditions as here main-
tain. Last Friday evening Lance phoned—I assumed it had to do with his weekend romp
with his kiddies—and when Ginger got off the
phone and returned to me in the living room
she looked a little glazed. "Lance is moving in
here for a while," she said.

I thought she was kidding. I offered a wide
sick smile like Steve Martin seeing a punchline,
and Ginger said, "I hope it won't be for long."

"Ha ha," I suggested, but I wasn't really
laughing. (I'd been in my living room chair,
with my after-dinner drink, reading Gore

Vidal's piece for *The Christmas Book,* and this return to the mundane world was a very difficult transition.) "Lance is not moving in here," I said.

"I'm afraid he is, Tom," she said, and sat in *her* chair, and told me about Helena and Santa Fe and the sublet. "The sublet starts the sixteenth," she finished, "next Monday, so Lance has to be out by then."

"He has to come *here*?"

"What am I going to do, Tom?" I could see then that she was at wit's end. Wringing her hands, she said, "It really isn't Lance's fault, I know it isn't, but it's *awfully* awkward."

"A similar phrase was going through my own brain."

"It's such short notice."

"It sure is."

"I meant for Lance," she said. "Helena didn't say a word to him until Tuesday—to avoid a fight, *she* said—just before she left."

"For Santa Fe."

"Lance spent the last three days trying to find an apartment, but you know what *that's* like in this city."

"It has been done."

"Not in three days. Not when you had no idea you were going to have to even *look* for an apartment."

"Granted," I said. "I still don't see . . ." I gestured encompassingly around our living room. *Our* living room.

"It's just for a little while," she said, "until

he can find a place. After all," she said, going on the attack slightly, "he *does* still pay part of the rent here."

If I'd had a beard, I would have muttered into it.

"And don't forget," she went on, "we're going to have *Mary* living with us for two weeks, out on Fire Island."

"In a completely separate house," I said. "And with plenty of advance warning. And I certainly don't *want* her there."

"Well, *I* don't want Lance *here*," she said, flaring a bit. "It could become very embarrassing. Besides, I think it could be bad for the children, seeing their father all the time."

"It could be bad for *me* seeing him all the time," I said. I smacked my chair arm. "Whose *chair* is this going to be? And that's another thing; you and he are still legally married, you know."

She narrowed her eyes. "Meaning what?"

"We're not going to get into any hassle about conjugal rights, are we?"

"Oh, don't be absurd!"

"All right, where's he going to sleep?"

"It'll have to be in your office, but it's just for a—"

"My office! I'm working full-time on *The Christmas Book*, I have material all over—"

"Lance won't be there except when he's asleep," she said, "and you won't be working in the middle of the night. You never did before."

"Work habits change."

"Oh, don't be silly."

"You're moving your *husband* into this apartment," I said, "and you're telling *me* not to be silly."

She sighed. She unnarrowed her eyes and bit her lower lip and looked honestly troubled. "I know, Tom," she said. "This is a terrible situation, nobody's happy about it, and I blame the whole thing on Helena."

"In Santa Fe."

"But what am I going to do?" she asked. "Lance spent three days trying to find some other solution, but there just isn't any. He wouldn't have called me if he'd had any other choice, and I wouldn't have said yes if *I'd* had any other choice."

"Move over," I said. "Let me up there with you on the no-other-choice shelf."

"It won't be that bad," she said.

"Oh, yes, it will. But as you say, there's nothing else to do."

"And it's only for a few days."

"Sure," I said, and Ginger came over and sat in my lap and thanked me for being understanding, and we kanoodled a bit.

So the next day, Saturday, Lance arrived to pick up his kids for the weekend, and when he brought them back on Sunday he stayed. Many suitcases and liquor store cartons filled up my office, the sofabed in there stood open, and Lance fell ravenously on the vodka when it was offered. He was looking pretty damn hangdog, and although I was goddam annoyed at the *situation*, I couldn't find it in my heart to be sore at Lance, so here we are with Lance living in what is, after all, his apartment. But at least he's had the grace to sit on the sofa and not my chair the few times he's been in the living room.

In truth, the idea of it is much worse than the actuality. Lance works in a midtown office—he's some sort of department head of a wholly-owned subsidiary of CBS that does blue-sky demographic research—and he's been arranging his dinners out in the world somewhere, so essentially we only see him for half an hour or so in the morning (he uses the kids' bathroom) and maybe a while in the evening. The arrangement is now four days old, and has been less awkward than one might have expected. Nevertheless, he is there, in my office.

And *The Christmas Book*, boxes and boxes of correspondence, tear sheets, Xeroxes, manuscripts, photos, tagged books, all of this compost that's supposed eventually to grow a mighty volume, has been laboriously moved from its proper home around my desk into this bedroom, where Ginger drapes her pantyhose over it. It's hard to take your life's work seriously when it's seen through a lot of double-layer crotches.

Despite it all, however, the book is coming along, with more and more terrific input from my celebs. The Gore Vidal piece I was reading when Lance broke over my bow was a weirdly effective and chilling item, half essay and half story, on the idea that what Christ brought to the world was not life but death. Pre-Christianity, if I understand what he's saying, was an innocent and happy pagan time because, although death existed, nobody cared much about its implications; instead, all living creatures devoted their attention to life. When Christ arrived, He brought with Him an obsession with death and what happens thereafter that darkened the world from His day till this. Makes a nice counterpoint to things like Garfield and the Coca-Cola tray.

Carl Sagan has sent me a hot-air balloon defining the star the Wise Men followed; sure, why not? And Stephen King came through with a cute twist-ending story about a little boy who sees future events in the shiny ornaments on the Christmas tree. Joan Didion, talking out of the side of her immobile mouth, sent along a cheery description of Christmas Eve on Los Angeles's Skid Row, and I *think* John Leonard's piece is about a marriage breaking up on Christmas morning. I *think* so.

On the visual side, Jules Feiffer sent along a nice strip of his dancer in her black leotard, plus a Santa Claus hat, doing a dance to Peace On Earth; she's dubious, but hopeful.

I'm not sure the Jill Krementz photo of the sidewalk Santas all gathered in a room to receive their instructions is exactly right for the book; somehow it's more reportage than what I'm looking for. I'm still thinking about that one. (I showed it to Mary, who can be very judgmental about successful photographers' work, and she regarded it with utter disdain. "Where's the *truth* in it?" she wanted to know. Her girl-builds-birdhouse series was rejected by that youth magazine, and rejection always makes her start talking about truth and esthetics and artistic purpose. Nevertheless, this time she may be right.)

The envelopes from Isaac Asimov I'm sending back unopened.

And now I have a letter from an agent named Henry Morrison, telling me his client, Robert Ludlum, had intended to do a Christmas short-short story for the book, but by the time he'd set the scene and introduced the characters he had twenty-five thousand words on paper, so it looks like it'll be his next novel instead— *The Yuletide Log*, perhaps—and therefore I shouldn't count on a submission from Ludlum. Less baroque refusals have been received from James Michener, William Styron and Pauline Kael, but with the depth on the bench I already have I'm no longer troubled by anybody saying no.

In fact, if it weren't for Lance in the house, I wouldn't have any troubles at all. (Apart from Mary, of course, weaving and unweaving Laërtes' winding sheet down there on West 17th Street, but that's something else.) The best news in a long long time is that good old Vickie managed the near-impossible: She got

Craig, Harry & Bourke to make a commitment and come up with the second payment
almost a month ahead of time! More than a
week ago, while I was still recovering from
Mother's Day, Vickie called to say she'd gotten Wilson to agree to the early pick-up. Our
delight was such that she left work early and
we had an immediate editorial conference to
celebrate.

Things continue very well on the Vickie front.
In fact, if the advent of Lance can be said to
have a silver lining, it is that it has given
Ginger enough to think about so she's less
likely to notice any little inadvertent clues I
may have on or about my person; like soap,
for instance.

But how much longer can this go on? The
situation is extremely fraught, I mean very
very densely fraught.

It is still very possible that this whole thing
will blow up in my face, and I'll lose everything: thrown out by Ginger, no more editorial conferences, and *The Christmas Book* at
the mercy of an editor who hates me.

In the meantime, before disaster comes—if
disaster is to come—Vickie and I are averag-
ing three conferences a week. She likes variety, Vickie does, drama, sweat, agony, fire-
works, sequential explosions. And then I come
home to Ginger, who expects to be treated
like the girl I left my wife for. It takes it out of
you. I mean it.

~~~~~~~~~~~~~~~~~~~~~~~~~~~

Friday, May 27th

I just delivered *The Christmas Book*!
Five days early!

Just this week I got my final little cluster of submissions, and they were all fine, and they brought the book up to a size where any more would be too much of a muchness, so I closed the giant doors. And the last through were some of the best.

Roddy McDowall's lovely pictures of celebrities giving their children Christmas presents, for instance, which arrived just barely in time for inclusion, make a very nice counterpoint right after Buckley's "Floating Celebration." (Even Mary couldn't find anything negative to say about those photos.) And until Paul Theroux sent in his grim and nasty piece about having a nervous breakdown alone in a motel room on Christmas Eve, far from one's family, I hadn't had anything that really *wonderfully* followed Dickens's "A Christmas Carol."

As for leading *in* to "A Christmas Carol," I had originally planned to use Galbraith's childhood-in-Canada reminiscence, but the Ann Beattie story I now have is much better for the job. In it, a young woman goes to three households on Christmas afternoon: her ex-husband's, who is married to a woman with two children and a St. Bernard; her current boyfriend's, he being a junior college English teacher endlessly planning to go live in Mexico; and her parents', they being retired but unwilling to move to Florida until they can believe their daughter is "settled." The story is called "Lies."

Let's see; what else? Russell Baker sent along a deceptively slight piece about the Christmas presents given and received during each of the Seven Ages of Man. It's funny and well observed, but also surprisingly sad when you stop to think about it. And from Calvin Trillin an oddity, a parody of a *New Yorker*-style local journalism piece, the kind of thing where *The New Yorker* goes to somewhere in South Dakota or North Carolina and does an in-depth but oblique piece about some fierce local controversy. In this one—"Journal: Bethlehem"—there are interviews with innkeepers and shepherds and Roman soldiers and the local gossipmonger, all on the ostensible subject of Herod's census but somehow circling around and around the birth of Christ. It's nicely done, but the strange thing is, of course, that Calvin Trillin himself is the one who does those things in *The New Yorker*. It isn't often a man parodies himself (at least not consciously), but I must say he did it well.

As for Mailer and Capote and their Death Row pieces, about a month ago I wrote both of them explaining the problem and saying that, while very different, both pieces were wonderful, and I would like their permission to run them both, with an editorial comment from me about how these two items show how *individual* true genius is. I said I wanted to run them one after the other—in my format they'll be about three pages each—either in alphabetical order or with their position determined by the toss of a coin or whatever method they would prefer.

Well. Both writers immediately *telephoned* me—an experience, let me tell you—demanding to see the other guy's work. I sent out Xeroxes with a request for a fast reading, and early this week I got approval from both; apparently, neither of them feels terribly threatened by the other. Capote did insist on alphabetical order, while Mailer suggested a refinement I rather like, which is to run the pieces *together*, on facing pages, with slightly different typefaces. So that's what I'm doing, with my own introductory comments on a right-hand page followed by six pages of their work, with Capote's piece on the left sides (to give him alphabetical precedence). A skimmer who reads it all as one six-page Death Row article will probably come away crosseyed, but that's okay.

With luck, this turning in of the manuscript will bring to an end, or at least give temporary respite from, another problem that's been getting increasingly tricky; namely, Ginger's desire to give dinner to my editor and her boyfriend. I've been stalling and dancing on that one, not even mentioning it to Vickie, although of course I do realize the eventual meeting is inevitable.

(Speaking of food and Vickie, while I am continuing to lose weight—nine pounds these last six weeks—Vickie is absolutely blooming. There had originally been a boniness about her that reminded me a little too specifically of the narrow-eyed lady waiting for me at home, but in the last few weeks she's become sleeker, just a bit fuller all over.)

In any event, after delivering the book I came home to find Lance already back from work (yes, he's still here, dammit; almost two weeks now), and he helped me shlep all the rest of the *Christmas Book* materials out of the bedroom and pile them in one corner of my office, near his cartons of stereo equipment and framed transparencies from *Fantasia*. Then he bathed in Brut and polished his bald spot to a high gloss and went hopefully out to a party (I'm using *hopefully* correctly there; hope I didn't confuse you). And now I'm waiting for Ginger to try on every garment she owns before we go out for our celebratory the-book-is-done-and-we've-spent-the-advance-dinner.

I wonder what I'll do next.

Tuesday, May 31st

LANCE and I are both in the doghouse with Ginger. What happened was, we got drunk. "Stinking drunk," in Ginger's felicitous and original phrase.

We have just had a long weekend, yesterday being Memorial Day, and long weekends are *hell* on separated daddies. You don't have the kids Saturday and Sunday, you have the kids Saturday and Sunday *and Monday*. They've seen the Central Park Zoo and the Bronx Zoo, they've seen the Empire State Building and the World Trade Center and the Statue of Liberty. The Staten Island ferry has ceased to enchant. Strolling around quaint neighborhoods like Chinatown and Greenwich Village is something your native New York kid *never* wants to do. Movies are over in less than two hours, and there you are on the sidewalk, and *now* what the hell?

To complicate matters, I now seem to have four weekend children instead of the standard two. Lance used to come obediently and take his away on Saturday and return them on Sunday, like everybody else, but now that he's living in the goddam apartment he no longer has to visit his children, so he doesn't. Also, the weekend is the best time for his two searches: an apartment, and a woman. It doesn't seem right to leave Joshua and Gretchen home alone when every other middle-class child in New York is out being entertained by daddy, so I've been bringing them along; the Brooklyn Botanic Gardens on Saturday to see the spring flowers, and the Cloisters on Sunday, because we hadn't been there for a while.

Yesterday, Monday, the traditional Memorial Day itself, I took the kids to lunch in a Columbus Avenue fern bar and then we walked down to one of the small movie houses near Lincoln Center to see some raunchy R-rated French film the kids wouldn't be allowed admittance to without the presence of a consenting adult, but when we got there that showing was sold out and there was no other movie in the neighborhood they all wanted to see. My capacity for invention had just reached overload, so we stood around on the sidewalk until Jennifer took pity on me and said, "Let's go home and play Uno." (*Home* has become a strange and slippery word these days, impossible to define except in context; in the circumstances of that moment, by "home" Jennifer meant my place on West End Avenue rather than her place on l7th Street, which everyone else automatically understood.)

So we went home, and Lance was there, wandering around stripped to the waist; which I thought was inappropriate. "I thought you were going apartment-hunting," I said.

"I've been," he told me. "No luck. I thought you were taking the kids to the movies."

I explained our misfortune, and went on to the bedroom to change out of my jacket, where I found Ginger, in a thoroughly bad mood for some reason, dressed in her robe and stripping the bed. "If you're going to change your *plans*," she said, "I wish you'd tell me. I intended to get a lot of cleaning done around here today."

"The movie was sold out."

Ginger banged open both bedroom windows. "Well, get out of *here*," she said. "I have to air this place out."

"It is a little musty," I agreed.

"Out."

Back in the living room, Lance apparently was feeling some belated sense of parental responsibility, because, having put a shirt on, he offered to join our little group and—since Ginger was, through various crashing noises deeper in the apartment, making it clear she didn't want any of us around right now—he even had a suggestion: "Let's go over to the park and do a little touch football, the Patchetts against the Diskants.''

Everybody thought that was a great idea. Bryan went to help Joshua clamber through his closet until he found his football, which was only slightly soft, and then we six left Ginger to her cleaning and her bad temper as we made our way eastward across 70th Street to Central Park, tossing the football back and forth along the way.

With frequent hilarity and many pauses and breaks and a few sidetrips to snack bars, we played a ridiculous game of touch football until nearly four-thirty. The Diskants won, eighty-four to thirty—we weren't doing extra points—primarily because every time Lance passed to Gretchen the ball was intercepted by Jennifer, who is very lithe and quick, with long skinny arms and the true competitive spirit. Gretchen began to look a little teary after a while, her underlip receding, so once or twice in our Diskant huddle I suggested to Jennifer she ease off the pressure, let Gretchen catch a pass or two—we did have a comfortable lead, after all—but Jennifer simply couldn't stop herself. Finally I deliberately threw a bad pass that *Gretchen* could intercept, and she ran with it for her only touchdown of the afternoon, which was enough to lift her spirits quite a bit.

Back at the apartment, there was a note from Ginger that she'd gone out shopping. I had to take my kids home, Gretchen and

Joshua immediately plunked themselves in front of the television set, and Lance volunteered to come along "for the ride," adding, "In fact, since my team lost, I'll spring for a cab."

"You're on," I said, and the children cheered.

The main reason I was pleased to have Lance along was as some protection from Mary, whose topics of conversation are invariably trouble. There's her career in photography, there's the subject of my moving back, there's the children's emotional condition, but the worst of all is sex.

This is increasing. Is it because she has no other sex life since I left? (*More* guilt.) Whatever the reason, we've reached the point now where every time she sees me she has another sexual encounter to describe, with friend or stranger. She can't take a subway without some man rubbing an erection against her. She can't go to a party without at least one male acquaintance subtly sliding his knee between her legs. She can't make a phone call or a purchase without somebody talking dirty to her.

I find all this disturbing. Well, naturally I do, because Mary is technically still my wife, after all, and nobody wants his woman—or his former woman—treated basely. But more than that, I don't want Mary *telling* me about it. She describes exactly the way it feels to be rubbed against in the subway, and how she knows the guy has had an ejaculation. She can remember every double entendre, every obscene gesture, every excuse this fellow or that fellow makes for touching her breast or her thigh or her behind. She never expresses an opinion about all this, never lets me guess if it frightens or angers or arouses her, but merely *describes* it all, as though she found it quite interesting and was sure I would, too.

I don't. Or, sometimes, I do, but that's worse. Of *course* I could go to bed with Mary, I know that, but then what? The whole point is, I've *left*, right? She's supposed to find a fella, get on with her life, ease my financial burden. We're separated, apart, it's *over*, she isn't supposed to look at me calmly with her clear blue eyes and tell me all these sex scenes. One way and another, it's, well, upsetting.

So that's why I was glad to have Lance along, which worked fairly well up to a point. That is, at least Mary didn't tell me about anybody coming in her pocket. She simply offered us coffee, which we both refused, but then she settled down to chat anyway, saying to Lance, "I understand you've moved back home."

"Well, not exactly," he said, grinning and looking uncomfortable. "You know about Helena. . . ."

"She went away, didn't she?"

"To Santa Fe," I said. For some reason, the choice of city still offended me.

"So you had to go home," Mary finished.

"I'm looking for a new place," Lance told

her. "Something small. Just a one-bedroom is all I need. If you hear of anything—"

"I'll be sure to call," Mary promised. To me, she said, "Tom, do you want to stay to dinner?"

She said that every time, ritually, and every time I gave her back the same ritual response: "No, thanks, I've got to get back uptown."

"With Lance up there," she said, going beyond ritual, "I thought you might be more comfortable down here."

Quickly, Lance said, "I'm going out for dinner. I don't, uh, I don't really *live* there."

"No, he doesn't," I said. "He just sort of sleeps there. In the office."

"Just until I can find an apartment."

"Tom? You don't have an office? How do you work?"

"I'm set up in the bedroom. It's fine," I said, annoyed to hear myself protesting too much.

"And it is only temporary," Lance said, also protesting too much.

"Very temporary," I protested.

"I'll be out of there any day now," Lance protested.

Before we became totally absurd, I stood and said, "I've really got to get uptown."

"Me, too," Lance said. But then he couldn't resist adding, "Uh, a different part of uptown."

Mary walked us to the apartment door, and as we were leaving she said, "Tom, if you need an office, your room is still here, you know. You could come down and work any time. Until Lance finds an apartment. Just temporarily."

Was she making fun of us? I decided to take it straight. "Thanks for the offer," I said. "I appreciate it."

Down on the sidewalk, Lance sighed and looked gloomy and said, "Mary still wants you, you know."

"Noticed that, did you?"

"It's nice to have somebody want you," he said. "Whether you want them or not."

"Rough out there, huh?"

"Oh, you don't know, Tom," he said, shaking his head. "You just don't know. And this last weekend, *Jesus*. The bitches I stand around talking to."

"Let's have a drink," I said.

Lance perked up a little at that, so we went over to Sixth Avenue and turned south and entered a bar, where we had a drink and Lance said, "I'm not a teenager any more, Tom, I don't like these goddam mating rituals. With Helena, I already knew her, I was leaving Ginger anyway, or she was leaving me, she'd already started on the side, you know. . . ."

"Absolutely not," I said. "Lance, it's water under the bridge, doesn't matter any more, but I absolutely swear you were already out of the house when Ginger and I got together."

"Oh, not you," he said, shrugging it away. "There were a couple of other guys before."

"Oh." I hadn't known about that.

"The point is," he said, "I was never in this goddam undignified position of *hunting* for a *woman*. It was all kind of like a square dance, everybody just moved one step over."

"Except Mary," I said bitterly.

He looked surprised. "That's right, isn't it? She never got hooked up with anybody else."

We were both silent then a minute, and I knew we were both thinking the same thought: Was Mary the solution to Lance's problem? Was Lance the solution to *my* problem?

No. I realized then for the first time that whenever I thought of Mary at last getting herself a fella, it was a given in my mind that it would be a fella *I didn't know*. The idea of Lance and Mary— No. "Incest" wasn't precisely the right word, but it had precisely the right feeling.

Lance's thoughts must have meandered to a similar terminus, because eventually he gave a long sigh, finished his drink, and said, "Let's find a better joint."

"You're right."

We crossed 14th Street into the Village, found another bar, and Lance told me about his experiences as a hunter of women: "They're *terrible*, Tom, there are a whole lot of truly terrible women out there, and they go to parties, and they *smoke*, and they have opinions about every goddam thing in the goddam world, and they're just making me very depressed."

We didn't like the jukebox in that place, so

we went on to another, and Lance told me more: "They have that magazine called *Self* for the single women," he said, "and believe me, Tom, the name tells it. The reason all those single women are single is not because nobody's noticed how terrific they are, it's because they *stink*."

"They do look good."

"That's part of the trouble," he said. "The one thing they believe in and truly understand is packaging. But you know what's inside the package?"

"Nothing," I guessed.

But he shook his head. "I'd take that. The way I feel right now, a woman with nothing at all inside her head would be a blessing. No, Tom; what's inside the package is *thoughts about the package*."

In the next bar, Lance told me about women whose lives were centered on jogging, and in the bar after that he told me what happens when you give up on all those self-centered Bloomingdale-wrapped single women and spend some time with a divorced woman instead: All *she* wants to talk about is her children. "I have children, too," he said. "*Everybody* has children, dammit, and my kids are just as neurotic and brilliant as their goddam kids, but I don't go around *talking* about it all the time."

The next bar was The Lion's Head, where there was a guy Lance knew and where I phoned Ginger, who sounded very cold and annoyed: "The children and I already ate."

"You did? What time is it?"

"Seven-twenty-three," she said, which meant she was in the bedroom with the digital clock. And it also meant she and the kids had eaten dinner earlier than usual.

"I'm sorry, Ginger," I said. "Lance and I just got to talking—"

"*Lance* and you! Oh, that's just too much," she said, and slammed the receiver down, and I went back to the bar to find that Lance had bought me a drink and was talking with his pal about television rating systems. It made for a change, so I joined in.

There was a party Lance was supposed to go to a little later, but he said he just couldn't face it. He thought he'd probably have dinner right there at The Lion's Head. I said I thought I would, too, since I seemed to be in the dog-house with Ginger. Lance shook his head and said, "That woman's got a lot of nerve."

During dinner, some other people we knew came in, and after dinner we went back to the bar where the group just kept getting larger, and we all kept finding things to laugh about, and then I have a sudden clear memory of the digital clock in the bedroom here reading three-twenty-seven in the dark. That was immediately followed by Ginger ruthlessly awakening me. It was morning, she claimed, and she was in an absolutely *rotten* mood.

What a way to start the day. Ginger yelled

at Lance and me all through breakfast, accusing us of male bonding. I don't know exactly where that phrase came from, but I suspect a woman must have made it up, deliberately choosing an expression that *sounds* painful. Women these days "network," a wonderfully mushy word that implies both serious business going on and yet a protective safety net below, but men are reduced to "bonding," something that sounds sticky and sadomasochistic. "Help me find the Krazy Glue, Ethel, I'm goin bondin' with the boys."

Anyway, having helped our hangovers no end, Ginger then stormed off to make her presence felt at work. A little later, Lance slunk away to his own work, and I was frowning at the bed, seriously contemplating a full day of sleep, when Vickie called to suggest an editorial conference. I told her I had a bad cold.

Fresh clean sheets.

Saturday, June 11th

WHAT a week; I never thought I'd get through it alive.

The trauma started on Tuesday, when Vickie called to say we were destined to have dinner together on Friday; *all* of us. It seems Ginger had tired of my inactivity and had made the Approach Direct, calling Vickie at work, identifying herself as "Tom's friend," and saying (according to Vickie), "We'd love to have you and *your* friend to dinner. Tom has just raved about how much help you've been on the book."

Spasms closed my throat when Vickie reported this, but I did manage to say, "What did you tell her?"

"What *could* I tell her? I was so startled all I could think to say was how delighted I'd be."

"Oh, boy."

"So we set a date for Friday."

"*This* Friday?"

"Of course. Tom, it'll be all right, don't worry about it."

"Who's going to be your friend?"

"I'll bring Carl along," she said.

Well. Carl Bindel is Vickie's secretary, a willowy boy in his late twenties with a sandy bushy moustache, large moist hazel eyes, spectacles with frames the same color as the moustache, and an absolutely terrifying sex life centered around various S-M bars in the West Village. There is absolutely no possible sexual permutation that could wind up with Carl and Vickie in a carnal relationship; it would be practically cross-species. Even Gretchen would take one look at those two and know they didn't hang out together, so the idea of Vickie passing off Carl as her boyfriend to Ginger would have been laughable if it weren't so horrifying. "Vickie!" I said. "*Carl?*"

"He can be very butch when he wants," she promised. "When his mother comes to New York, for instance. Besides, I already asked and he said yes. He'll do just fine. He says it'll be a hoot."

"Uhh, Vickie," I said, "maybe you should suggest that he not call anything a hoot during dinner."

"He'll do just *fine*, Tom," she insisted. "Are we still on for our conference tomorrow?"

"You bet," I said, but faintly.

The rest of the week, apart from editorial conferences, I spent working on a couple of magazine pieces to pay the rent, trying to get them out of the way before the copy-edited *Christmas Book* comes back, which will be any day now. Unfortunately, it seems impossible to get *Lance* out of the way, so I'm still working in the bedroom, which is all right for now, but once *The Christmas Book* returns this room is going to get awfully crowded.

The problem is, since Lance hasn't found an apartment yet and we're going to be out on Fire Island all next month anyway, it's been agreed he'll stay here through July. He absolutely swears and vows and promises he'll have made some other arrangement by August first, but in the meantime his interest in both of his searches—a place to live and a new girlfriend—seems to have slackened considerably. He's spending more and more evenings at home, and is now an apparently permanent addition to my weekend jaunts with the kids.

In fact, he joined us for dinner Friday, which did nothing to normalize an already weird occasion. Ginger came home from work early Friday afternoon to start cooking, while I stayed in the bedroom, trying to concentrate on my final draft of the "Major Jewels in History" piece *Cosmopolitan* had commissioned, and when Lance arrived at five-forty-eight by the digital clock, I abandoned the

Hope and the Kohinoor and the rest of them and joined him for a prehurricane drink.

I had not, of course, confided in Lance about my carrying-on with Vickie—there's just no way to tell a man you're cheating on his wife—so it was impossible to enlist his aid in the ordeal to come. While Ginger chopped and poured and pounded in the kitchen, Lance and I sat in the living room and chatted of inessentials, and my drink just seemed to vanish; so I had another.

Vickie and her friend had been invited for seven. Believing that whatever wits I had I should keep about me, I stopped after the second drink and just sat in the living room, smiling and nodding and listening to Lance's incomprehensible shoptalk about CBS executive politics, while inside I felt exactly the way I used to as a child at the dentist's: I don't care how awful it is, just so it's *over*.

A little after seven, fashionably late, the downstairs bell rang. Going to the intercom in the front hall, I asked who it was, and a voice said, "Vickie and Carl." I smiled grimly, realizing I didn't know which of them had answered, and buzzed them in.

Ginger removed her apron, dried her hands and was standing smiling in the living room, all her hundreds of eyes very wide-open and glinting, when the upstairs bell rang and I opened to the happy couple. "Hi, Vickie. Hiya, Carl." Vickie and I leaned forward to kiss the air beside one another's cheeks; she smelled

like illicit afternoons. Smiling, Carl extended
a scrod fillet and I gave it a manly shake and
he winced, but happily. "Come on in," I said,
against my urgent desire to scream GO AWAY
FOREVER!, and shepherded them into the
living room for introductions.

Both guests were dressed a bit oddly. Vickie
had apparently decided to allay suspicion by
appearing as a frump, because she was wearing black pantyhose and a dark paisley-pattern
dress that was too tight for her, emphasizing
bumps and rolls I'd never noticed before. As
for Carl, his tight designer jeans were tucked
into his high-heeled cowboy boots, and his
canary yellow shirt under a fringed tan suede
jacket was graced by a black string tie. His
belt buckle, shaped like a large rectangular
manhole cover, had a bucking bronco on it.

I introduced everybody to everybody else.
The fact that Ginger and Lance had the same
last name made Vickie pause a millisecond,
but then she sailed onward and I'm sure I was
the only one who noticed. She said to Ginger,
"Something smells *delicious*."

"I *hope* it'll be all right. It's a new recipe
from Elizabeth David."

"Isn't she *fantastic*? Can I do anything to
help?"

"No, no, I have everything under control. I
think."

Meantime, I was singing my part: "Can I
offer anyone a drink?"

I could. Drinks were made, Vickie joined

Ginger in the kitchen, and we three hearty males sat around the living room listening to our horses eat hay and the lonely cry of a distant old coyote. Lance broke a rather painful silence by saying, to the room at large, "What do you think's going to happen to the Mets this year?"

"Oh, the Lord knows," Carl said, waving airy fingers. "With Bliss gone, it's a whole new ballgame."

Lance gave him a puzzled look. "Bliss?"

"Anthony Bliss," Carl said. "The general manager."

Lance was floundering. "Of the *Mets*?"

"Of the Met, yes." Looking to me for confirmation, Carl said, "Anthony Bliss." Turning back to Lance he said, "Of course, if they replace him with another Beverly Sills, *quelle* disaster."

"Opera," I said, catching up. "The Metropolitan Opera."

"Well, yes, of course." Belatedly, Carl too was becoming puzzled. "What else were we talking about?"

"Baseball," I said.

"The New York Mets," Lance said, with some emphasis.

"Oh, *base*-ball!" Carl did his airy wave again. "Macho ballet," he said.

Apparently, Vickie and Ginger were hitting it off somewhat better in the kitchen, so that by the time we sat down to our meal at least the women were relaxed. (Joshua and Gretchen had both been farmed out for a few hours, Gretchen dining at a school chum's house, Joshua downtown with Mary and my kids. He would sleep over, and I would pick the whole crew up—sans Mary—in the morning.) We talked publishing gossip mostly during dinner, that being the one subject that could reach all the way from Carl to Lance, Carl for the evening pretending to be another editor at Craig rather than Vickie's secretary. (One pretense among so many.) A few times I saw Ginger give Carl a puzzled look, but that was all.

After dinner I went to the kitchen to make more drinks, and all at once Vickie was in the doorway, a devilish grin on her lips and a sparkle in her eyes as she hissed, "A *ménage à trois?*" (I know there are those who claim you can't hiss a word without an S in it, but that's nonsense. In human speech, to hiss is to whisper forcefully. Pooh to Newgate Callendar.)

At any rate, I was both startled and alarmed. "No, no," I whispered. (Not being forceful, it wasn't a hiss.) "Lance is just between apartments, that's all. There's *nothing* going on."

"I've never done that," she mused, and gave another wicked smile. "I'd like to be a sandwich!"

"With Carl?"

She raised her eyes to heaven. "He can be the lettuce leaf," she said, and went away to the living room.

Mercifully, it was an early evening; one postprandial drink and a brief description by Carl of a Bette Midler stage show he'd recently seen (complete with impersonations), and they were off, Carl a cowgirl Ariel and Vickie in her too-tight frowsy dress a lonely Caliban. At least he hadn't described anything as a hoot.

Later, in bed, Ginger employed the phrase "fag hag." I blinked big innocent eyes: "What?"

"Well, surely it's obvious. Carl is gay as a jay."

"I thought he was a little—ambiguous," I admitted.

"Ambiguous? I thought he'd go down on the candelabra!"

"Vickie's never talked about him much," I said, shrugging it off.

Unsuccessfully. "That's because she's probably embarrassed," Ginger said. "But she's your typical fag hag; afraid of sex, afraid of adult relationships, so she wears frumpy, unattractive clothes and just hangs out with faggots. Did you see that *dress?*"

"Yes, I did," I admitted. I felt I should be defending Vickie somehow, but there was just no way to do it. And wasn't this, under the circumstances, the best possible view for Ginger to take of Vickie? Nevertheless, I couldn't resist adding, "I thought you two got along."

"We did," Ginger said. "As a woman, I think she's very sensible. But can you actually believe she's having an *affair* with Carl?"

"I guess not," I said.

"Does she dress that way in the office?".

"I don't know, I suppose so, I never noticed that much. Not come-on, anyway."

Suddenly Ginger's eyes were narrowed, and peering at me. "No," she said.

"No what?"

"Not come-on. Did you like the ratatouille?" *Quelle* (as Carl would say) change of subject. I complimented her on dinner for a while, and we never did return to the topic of Vickie, so I didn't find out what had been going on inside her head for that one tiny instant.

This afternoon—being the day after—I had another brief and equally disquieting talk about Vickie, this one with Lance, in the Central Park Zoo, while the children amused themselves making faces at the monkeys. (The boys always want to look at the snakes, the girls always want to look at the cats, and they always compromise by looking at the monkeys.) "That editor of yours," Lance said.

"Oh?"

"Is that *really* her boyfriend?"

"Lance, I have no idea," I said. "Ginger invited her to dinner, and that's who she brought."

"Good-looking woman," he said, staring at the monkeys, who were making faces at one another. "She doesn't know how to wear clothes, but that isn't everything."

I thought I saw where his thoughts were trending, and I didn't like it. "She *was* kind of frumpy," I said. "Ginger thinks she's a fag hag."

But he wasn't to be deflected that easily. "Oh, I don't think so," he said, nodding, musing, pondering. "There's a real woman inside there. Maybe she's on the rebound or something."

"That's possible."

"I don't suppose you know her home number?"

"Sorry," I said.

"We've already been introduced, last night," he reminded himself. "I could call her at work."

"Yes, you could," I said.

Now what? Lance and Vickie? To solve the Lance problem must I recreate the *Christmas Book* problem? Is nothing to be simple any more, ever again?

Thursday, June 30th

IT'S not that I'm a nervous traveler. It's just that I'm all packed and ready, and we aren't leaving until tomorrow.

June has gone by in a blur. All of a sudden *The Christmas Book* is a major issue in my life again, and I've spent most of the last two weeks in an empty office down at Craig, Harry & Bourke, going over the copy-edited manuscript, straightening out worldwide copyright problems with the rights department, arguing with production about the quality of the first trial color pages (we have thirty-two, done in some new process that doesn't look quite as cheap as it is), and generally behaving like an executive. Also, Vickie and I have managed to perform a few natural and unnatural acts in there, keeping one eye on the door.

Time has suddenly become a major problem. Craig wants books in the stores by the end of October, which in publishing terms is yesterday. What with the urgency involved, plus the unwieldy size and shape of the manuscript itself, plus all the other details to be seen to, it just made more sense for Mohammed (me) to go to the mountain (the ms). Also, having an office full of Lance and a bedroom full of flung pantyhose didn't help.

Because of the hurry, and because of the size of the book, they didn't wait for the copyediting phase to be finished before sending the manuscript off to the typesetter, but sent it on in batches, and the first batch of galleys should be returning any day for me to proofread. In the meantime, just yesterday I finished the *Cosmo* jewel piece and mailed it to my editor there and have been finishing a piece for *Geo*; but with this imminent move to Fire Island it just hasn't been possible to think about the wonderful ancient Mayans of Belize. I'll finish the piece next week, out there.

Lance has dated Vickie two or three times, but I haven't been able to get a straight answer from either of them as to precisely what this means. I don't think they've been to bed together, or Lance would certainly have told me. Lance hasn't mentioned anything about Vickie to Ginger, which I guess is just as well; it's probably better for Ginger to go on thinking of Vickie as a fag hag.

I am looking forward to comparative peace and quiet; not tomorrow, when we make the big move, but starting the day after. With Vickie here and me out there, editorial conferences will quite naturally be fewer, though *The Christmas Book* will of course require at least my occasional presence in New York. But even with Mary hanging around the first two weeks, I am anticipating a simpler and more comprehendable existence for the next month.

As for tomorrow, the simplest and almost the least expensive method for transporting all these people and luggage turns out to be a rented station wagon, with driver. He is due to arrive at 17th Street tomorrow morning at ten, to pick up Mary and Bryan and Jennifer and all their goods and chattels, then come uptown to get me, plus Joshua and Gretchen and *this* pile of baggage, which includes my typewriter and a liquor store carton filled with work necessities, such as pencils and a thesaurus. Also a carton full of sandwiches and apples and tomato juice and vodka. If the traffic on Long Island treats us decently, we'll make the 1:00 ferry and have a picnic lunch in the rented house, and Ginger will leave work early and be on the 5:00 ferry. (She surprised me by very graciously accepting Mary's offer to make dinner for everybody tomorrow night.) The weather is expected to be sunny and mild.

I can't help wondering what will go wrong.

LATER

Good God. Vickie just called. The galleys for
the first quarter of the book, exclusive of artwork, will arrive at Craig from the typesetter
in Pennsylvania some time tomorrow afternoon. Vickie has volunteered—there was simply no way I could say no—to bring them out
to Fire Island on Saturday.

I am to go over the galleys, according to
this plan, while Vickie sunbathes the weekend away. On the afternoon of Monday, the
Fourth of July, she will carry the corrected
galleys back to New York; mission accomplished. I did explain that we were already
pretty crowded out there, but she said that
was okay, she didn't mind, she'd bring a sleeping bag and just bunk on the living room
floor.

This is insane. Where do you go to enlist in
the Foreign Legion? I am going to be in that
small rented house over the Fourth of July
weekend with Mary *and* Ginger *and* VICKIE!
What kind of Independence Day do you call
that?

~~~~~~~~~~~~~~~~~

Sunday, July 3rd

AND it isn't even over.

I was seated on the back deck a little while ago, reading the Sunday *Times* Magazine, and then I looked around at the three other people also on the deck, also reading sections of the *Times*, and I found myself thinking: I have been to bed with all three of these women.

The thought did not make me feel like a harem master or anything particularly macho. In fact, all I felt at that moment was vaguely scared. Three women in bikinis in the sunshine, reading Travel and Arts and Leisure and The Week in Review. If they were suddenly to rise and turn on me, they could tear me to shreds. Sitting there, looking at them, thinking about it, I could find no very good reason why they *wouldn't* rise and turn on me. Dropping the Magazine—I hadn't found the rift between the French Newer Left and the Roman Catholic Church all that fascinating anyway—I rose and announced in a loud confident voice that I really ought to do some more work on the galleys of *The Christmas Book*. Then I fled away up here to Ginger's and my bedroom, where I have made a fairly useful desk out of a closet door lying across plastic milk crates stacked two high. We don't particularly need a door on the closet up here anyway. (The knobs are at the back.)

One thing we hadn't foreseen in April, when we rented the place, was that in the summer this upstairs room would be an absolute oven in the daytime. I may have to buy a fan, if I'm going to do much work up here. In the meantime, baking here in the heat is still better than sitting down there among my women.

From time to time I glance out the window at them, still all sprawled there, legs stretched out on the webbed chaise longues, sunglasses on faces, strategic bits of colored cloth interrupting the flow of flesh. A smell of rancid coconut rises from the suntan oil that makes that flesh so prettily gleam. From time to time they turn a page or exchange sections of the paper. Periodically Vickie rolls over onto her stomach, to sun her back, but is never comfortable that way and soon rolls back again. The only good thing I can say about the scene is that at least they aren't talking to one another.

Am I a misogynist? Am I one of those men

who claim to love women but who secretly hate and fear them? Am I guilt-ridden? Do I feel I *deserve* to be torn limb from limb by a shock of bikini-clad avengers?

Uhh, actually, no. Everything would be fine, perfectly normal, if it weren't for the addition of Vickie. No matter how trapped I am, no matter how justified in the whole Vickie thing, Ginger would be *very* upset if she found out about it. When Ginger was The Other Woman, it was a very straightforward role; I was falling out of that previous nest, and she was passing by underneath. But now Ginger is simultaneously The Other Woman *and* The Wronged Woman, and debased in both roles.

As for Mary, the one thing that has kept our relationship relatively smooth has been her belief that I have *tried to be honorable*. Failed sometimes, but at least tried. One of the reasons she wants me back is that she thinks I'm a decent guy. If she found out about Vickie, it would remove the dignity from the ending of our marriage; I would have proved myself unworthy to have left her.

Whereas, if Vickie were to discover her main attraction for me was bookish rather than bawdy, she'd lead the posse.

My women.

Monday, July 4th

I'M a nervous wreck.

Of *course* Vickie would demand sex while she was here. She gave me several high-signs yesterday, once the heat in the bedroom had driven me back downstairs, but with two other adults and four children about the place all day Sunday it just wasn't possible. And I'd assumed it would go on being impossible.

But then came today. The beach is seven houses and a dune from here, and after breakfast everybody went there, leaving me to finish my work on the galleys before the bedroom becomes too hot to stand, and so Vickie could take them back to the city with her this afternoon. Suddenly, a little before eleven, here came Vickie skipping into the bedroom, smiling her lascivious smile and untying her strings. "Oh, no!" I said, but, "We've got time," she assured me, giggling.

We did, too, but only just. She had barely managed to reassemble herself and be in the kitchen making a big quart bottle of packaged lemonade when Ginger arrived. "Oh, dear," I heard Vickie say. "I wanted to surprise you."

"Mmm," said Ginger's voice. "How's Tom doing?"

"Sore as a bear," Vickie told her. "I guess those galleys are driving him crazy. I called up to him, but he just growled."

So Ginger didn't come upstairs to inspect the site of the skirmish, and soon both women went back to the beach with the bottle of iced lemonade and a handful of plastic cups, and I went to take my second shower of the day.

But not my last. At lunchtime everybody descended, including me carrying the finished galleys in their big sloppy envelope, and we sat around the table on the deck, under the big beach umbrella, making cold cut sandwiches and drinking white wine spritzers. (The children stuck to lemonade.)

After lunch, Vickie went off to Jennifer and Gretchen's room to change, while Mary and the kids went back to the beach, Mary wearing a bikini and two cameras, with a third camera in the canvas bag she carried, down among the suntan oils and paperback books and crumpled tissues. Then Ginger and I walked Vickie to the dock, where she and the galleys took the three-ten ferry and life became slightly more plausible.

Walking back to the house, Ginger gave me an updated assessment of Vickie, making several negative observations with which I wholeheartedly agreed. Then she said, "How do you feel, surrounded by all these women?"

"Like an Oriental potentate," I said.

She considered that, as though it had been a real answer, then said, "Really?"

"Not really. For one thing, I don't have my pick of the harem."

"You're damn right you don't." Then she linked her arm with mine and gazed around at the day and said, "It's beautiful out here."

"It sure is."

"I hate having to go back to work."

"It's only one week," I pointed out. Ginger had had to pull some strings and request special favors to get most of July off, and at that she couldn't wangle the entire month. Next week, from the eleventh till the fifteenth, she'll have to commute, getting up every morning to take the 7:15 ferry—locally known as the "Death Boat"—then returning on the 6:05; the "Daddy Boat," though not in this case.

"I don't like leaving you here alone," she said.

"I won't be alone. I'll have the kids. And Mary."

"That's what I don't like about it."

"Oh, come on, Ginger," I said. "Don't try to tell me you're jealous of Mary."

"She wants you back."

"Granted."

"She'll work her wiles on you when I'm gone."

"Mary doesn't have any wiles," I said.

She laughed, and disengaged her arm from mine. I said, "Don't get mad for no reason."

Brooding, she said, "Sometimes I'd like to know what a man thinks about."

"Sex."

She nodded. "Good idea."

So it was back up to the bedroom we went. It must have been way over ninety in there by then, but did that stop us? Unfortunately not.

So there I was, engaged in perfectly legitimate intercourse with my mistress, while my wife was up at the beach and my girlfriend was off on the 3:10, when all of a sudden a perfectly awful *noise* threw the both of us off-stride and then some. It sounded like a cat fight, it sounded like mongooses mating, it sounded like a beached whale, it sounded like the death-cry of an elk, it sounded like ... I don't know what it sounded like.

But, looking out the window, I found out what it *was.* It was Bryan, blowing into the clarinet he'd been given last Christmas. I've been paying for lessons, of course, and Mary had told me he was being fairly diligent with his practice, but since I don't actually live with the kid I'd never heard these terrible sounds before, so naturally I screamed out the window, *"Bryan! For God's sake!"*

He stopped squawking, looked up at me, and smiled happily. "That's *Jingle Bells*," he said.

"The hell it is! Take that thing off into the sand dunes somewhere if you're going to play it! Take it to Atlantique!"

Behind me, Ginger was saying, "Don't discourage him, Tom, let him play."

"Play!" I yelled at her. "You call that play?"

"I don't get to practice anywhere," Bryan complained on my other flank. "How am I going to grow up to be Artie Shaw?"

Where did he ever hear of Artie Shaw? And why on Earth would he want to grow up to be him? "Take—that—*away*!" I yelled, pointing toward Europe.

So he moped off, clarinet at half-mast, body doing a whole great exaggerated number on how mournful he felt. Clarinet! *That's* what Christmas is!

Meantime, Ginger was nagging, saying, "That's no way to act toward a child who's taking an *interest* in something."

"Under this window?"

"You could have spoken to him gently and reasonably."

"I didn't feel gentle and reasonable."

"You certainly didn't."

So much for sex; we spent the time instead arguing about me mistreating my children. Well, it made a change from our argument about me mistreating *her* children.

Wednesday, July 13th

STABBED!
  Betrayed!
  Bewildered.
  There must be a logical sequence of events here. The *events* are by no means logical, but maybe the sequence can become so.
  At about ten-thirty this morning, with me deep in the Central American rain forests among the Mayans, Vickie phoned. She bandied no words, but got to the point at once. "Hello, Tom," she said. "I'm pregnant."
  "Oh, my God!"
  "Don't worry, it isn't you," she said, sounding somewhat bitter.
  "It isn't? Who is it?"
  "Well, that's the problem," she said. "You and I met the end of March, and the doctor says I was already pregnant then, and the

way the timing works it must have been the last week in February, right after Washington's Birthday. That's when I took a week off and went to Club Med."

"Oh."

"So that's that," she said.

I said, "Wait a minute. Vickie, you're *four and a half months* pregnant, and you didn't know it?"

"Well, I've always been very irregular," she said. "My GYN says it's a neurotic reaction. I just thought, well, I'm crazier than usual because I'm fucking a writer."

Letting that one pass, I said, "So what now?"

"Well, it's too late for an abortion. I'm going to Fort Lauderdale, talk it over with my mother, brood about things. I may keep the kid, if it's fairly attractive."

"How long—" My voice failed me, because I suddenly saw why she was phoning. "How long will you be gone?"

"That's hard to say. Depends on a lot of things. I'm asking for a year's absence. Without pay, of course. Let my mother support me, the nasty bitch."

"You aren't my editor any more," I said.

"I'm sorry about that, Tom," she said. "There's a couple books I'm really sorry to leave behind, and that's one of them. I enjoyed working with you. You know, the fucking too, but also the book. It's nice to work with a professional."

"Thank you," I said, while my other hand

crumpled mounds of paper. *This* is why she's been gaining weight!

"I'll stay on till the end of the week," she said. "Don't worry, I'll see they give you to somebody good."

There is no such thing. I said, "Not the man who edits the war books?"

"Funny thing about Hiram," she said. "He died last month."

"Hilarious."

"Died at his desk. Apparently he was there three or four days, nobody noticed. Finally one of the cleaning women one night, vacuuming around him, she noticed the smell."

"Well, somebody goes and somebody comes."

"It's been nice coming with you, Tom. I don't suppose you'll be in the city the next few days."

"Sorry," I said. "I'm all tied up out here."

"Ah, well. Maybe next year sometime."

"Maybe so," I said.

"So long, Tom," she said.

"So long. Say hello to your mother."

"I suppose I'll have to," she said, and that was that.

Well, that ended the Mayans for today. Even though I'd heard Mary moving around downstairs, I abandoned my desk and my privacy at once, too shaken to worry about what she might want to say to me.

The problem is, out here in the humid sunny heat, with everybody damn near naked anyway, Mary's sexual encounters are getting steamier and steamier, and she just insists on *telling* me about them. "There was a man up at the beach in one of those very skimpy swimsuits," she said the other day, "sitting on a towel facing me with his knees up and his legs spread. He kept looking at me, and sort of running his fingers up and down his own thigh, like this—" She showed me, running her own fingers up and down her own thigh, not quite to the swimsuit-covered crotch. "—and I could see he was getting an erection. Well, I—"

"Mary, I don't need to know all—"

"It's so *different* out here," she went on, blandly, merely interested in her own story. "People wear so little, and they just let you see everything that's happening to them. And this man's suit was that very thin kind of shiny material—you know the kind I mean?"

"Yes, Mary, I—"

"I could see *everything*," she told me, calm eyes round and innocent. "And it was a very thick one, too. But not too long, which was lucky, or it would have poked right out the top of the suit."

"Mary, look, you—"

"And then he came over to ask me what time it was. I was sitting on the beach towel, you know, and he stood right next to me, and there it was, practically in my face. I could see the *vein*. And he said, 'Do you have the time?' And I said, 'No, I don't have my watch with me,' and then he smiled and sort of *gyrated*, like this." And she did a slow round movement with her hips. She's in very good physical condition, Mary, the muscles rippling beneath the flesh as she did a deliberate illustrative bump and grind.

"Mary," I said firmly, "if you wouldn't look *back* at these people, they—"

"They'll just come over," she said. "It's because I'm alone. This man, I just told him, 'I'm going for a swim now,' and I did."

"So am I," I said, and went away and leaped directly into the water, which steamed around me.

That wasn't the only one, not by a long shot. Almost every day, Mary has another rutting male to tell me about. There was the time she was body-surfing and a man nearby, also body-surfing, kept managing to bump into her in the water, once getting his hand inside her bra. And the man who tried to adjust her bicycle seat while she was seated on the bicycle. And the man with the banana, who—

Well. The point is, for my own peace of mind I've been avoiding Mary as much as possible while Ginger's away in town, this being the week Ginger has to commute. (Mary won't tell these stories in front of Ginger, of course.) But today was a special case if there ever was one, and so, regardless of what pornography awaited me below, I went downstairs after my Vickie conversation, and into the kitchen, where Mary was boiling water for iced tea. I took a glass down from the shelf, put ice cubes in it from the freezer, then filled it about halfway with vodka. I had opened the refrigerator door and was reaching for the orange juice when Mary said, "Tom? Is something wrong?"

"You remember Vickie Douglas," I said, pouring orange juice.

"Your editor, yes."

"She's pregnant," I said, putting the orange juice away.

"Tom!" She stared at me.

"Not by *me*," I said in irritation, and knocked back half my drink. Then another ramification of the situation came to me—the realization that that irregular madwoman was capable of getting herself knocked up at her age despite all the aids and counsel of modern-day science, and if she hadn't been preggers already when we'd met I *could* have been the father—and I knocked back the drink's other half.

"Tom, it's ten-thirty in the morning," Mary said.

"You gonna tell me the sports next?"

"I don't understand," she said. "What's the problem?"

"Vickie is taking a year's leave of absence. She is no longer my editor. *The Christmas Book* is an orphan."

"Well, that happened before," she pointed out, "when Jack Rosenfarb left. You were worried then, and it worked out all right with Vickie."

"That was a special case," I muttered. I was building a second drink. It would simply not be possible for me to climb into bed with Hambleton Cudlipp the Third. Nor could I see myself running this whole routine again if they gave me another Vickie Douglas, of whom there is a rich supply in New York publishing. "I'm doomed," I said.

The whistling teakettle whistled. Mary made tea while I made a screwdriver and took it out to the back deck. Standing in the sunshine, I surveyed the blackness of life. Mary came out and touched my arm and said, "It'll be all right, Tom."

"It will not. We are precisely at the point where Craig can drop the ball." I nodded at the little guesthouse. "How's the accommodation?"

"Fine," she said. "Hot in the daytime, but I'm never in there in the daytime. Tom, don't brood."

"The definition of insanity," I said, "is 'an inappropriate reaction to stimuli.' Given the stimuli I've just been hit with, if I *didn't* brood I'd be crazy." I swigged screwdriver.

Mary took the glass out of my hand and put it on the table. "Don't hurt yourself, Tom," she said. "It isn't your fault."

"*I* know that."

"So don't make it worse. You'll give yourself a headache and a hangover and an upset stomach, you'll ruin the entire day—"

"The entire day *is* ruined."

She came over and put her arms around me and drew my head down into the crook of her shoulder and throat. Patting the back of my head, holding my torso with her other arm, she murmured, "It'll be all right. It'll be all right."

Mary is several inches shorter than me, so it was a somewhat awkward posture I was in, knees bent slightly, head folded down like a hanging victim, and yet a sudden wave of comfort and warmth flowed over me as I stood there, much stronger and sweeter than anything the vodka could have done. Mary was in her bikini and my hands felt the warmth of her back. In my nose was a faint aroma, a sweet duskiness, that reminded me of times long long ago.

When a couple live together for years, they lose the knowledge of one another's scent. But Mary and I had been apart now for seventeen months, and had become strangers again. Her fragrance was both new and old—and so was the feel of her body against me—and very disturbing.

She stopped patting my head, but continued to hold me, and arched her back so she could look up at my face. "Are you all right?"

"I'll survive," I said, and kissed her.

Very warm. The old-and-new again. Known but exotic. Complex. Memory and desire and regret and distant warning bells.

She released me, stepped back, smiled. If she had smiled in some sort of triumph or conquest I would have hated her, but there was nothing in the smile but care and concern. "Sit down," she said, "I'll make coffee."

I sat under the beach umbrella, looking out at the sunlight. My thoughts were confused, but calmer. The problems of *The Christmas Book* seemed very far away; important, but not urgent.

I did not go to bed with Mary, nor did she seem to assume I might. If there had been any hint of it from her, would I have followed through? I have no idea.

The coffee helped, and further calm conversation with Mary helped, but I still got my headache. Now I shall go fling myself into the ocean.

Sunday, July 17th

MARY left this afternoon.

Several times in the last two weeks I thought the situation might explode, but it never quite did happen. Ginger once or twice *wanted* an explosion, and I could see it, and I guess Mary could see it, too, because she very gently and quietly disappeared from view. I made the mistake once of pointing this out to Ginger: "You keep saying Mary's devious," I said, "but if she was devious wouldn't she let you pick a fight with her?"

"What do you mean, pick a fight?"

"You've been spoiling for a fight all—"

Well. That was a mistake, which took about a day and a half to rectify.

Otherwise, both women were rather good about it. They went to the beach together— with all the kids—and they talked together civilly enough. There was tacit agreement that Ginger was boss of the kitchen and Mary a guest eating Ginger's meals, except that the five days Ginger had to go to work in the city Mary volunteered to make dinner and Ginger accepted the offer. Every evening, if we weren't all playing a boardgame or something with the kids, Mary would retire to her guesthouse and read while Ginger and I did whatever we did in the main house.

Fair Harbor on Fire Island is a very communications-biz community, with television people and ad agency people as well as writers and editors and a sprinkling of showfolk. I know a few of these people, mostly through business contacts, and one of the guys, a magazine editor named Herm Morgenstern who by summer is a feared and ruthless volleyball player—he finishes most summers absolutely swathed in Ace bandages—said to me on the beach one day, grinning, "Tom, I don't know how you do it."

"Do what?"

"The women." He shook his head in admiration. "Jeezuz. The wife *and* the girlfriend, all in the same house. You all bunk in together, do you?" His tongue was somewhat hanging out.

"Hey, no," I said. "It's nothing like that at all, Herm. Mary and I are *separated*, she has her own little guesthouse, there's nothing going on at all."

"Sure," he said, nodding, smirking. "Sure."

I was reminded of Vickie assuming Ginger and Lance and I had a *ménage à trois*, and I imagine Herm wasn't the only person in Fair Harbor making the same assumption about Ginger and Mary and me. I suppose other people's lives always look more exciting; it's hard to believe that *everybody's* as disorganized and screwed-up and ordinary as ourselves.

It's funny, but the place feels incomplete without Mary prowling around, hung with cameras, looking for not-quite-good-enough photo opportunities. A few empty film containers are still to be seen here and there, little black plastic jars with gray plastic tops, and they remind me of her; Mary's need to be a successful photographer, Mary's softness that makes the goal impossible.

Why did all that make her somehow belong here? I don't know. I only know we'd established a status quo here, the seven of us, against all odds, and now I find myself missing it. Afraid I might make the mistake of letting Ginger see the way I feel, I have come up to the evening-cooled bedroom to work on the second batch of *Christmas Book* galleys. Last Friday, Vickie, in her final official act before motherhood—if that kid is smart, it'll leave the womb running—messengered this second portion of the galleys over to Ginger's office, and Ginger brought them out with her that evening, and I've been working on them ever since.

There wasn't time to correct them all before Mary's departure today, unfortunately, or she could have taken them with her. Somehow I'll have to get them back to Craig this week.

I wonder who I'll address them to?

~~~~~~~~~~~~~~~~~~~~~~~~~~

Tuesday, July 19th

I knew Dewey Heffernan was trouble when he phoned yesterday to introduce himself. "This is Dewey Heffernan," said a voice so young and eager my first thought was that this at last was Jennifer's first boyfriend, an advent we've all been anticipating with some suspense, and not a little dread. But, no; Jennifer was apparently still prepubescent, because *this* Dewey Heffernan was to be my new editor.

The publishing world contains more disasters than are dreamt of in your philosophy, Huck.

"I'm really excited about this, Tom," Dewey Heffernan said, while I stood with the phone in my Fire Island living room in my swimsuit and Earth Day T-shirt and slowly died. "May I call you Tom?"

You may not call me at all, fella. "Sure," I said.

"And I hope you'll call me Dewey."

"I will," I promised.

"I just want you to know," he said, "when Miss Douglas told me I was going to take over *The Christmas Story* I just—"

"*The Christmas Book*," I said.

"I've loved Christmas since I was a little kid," he assured me. "This is the *most* exciting thing that's happened to me on this job."

"Mmm," I said.

Dewey was calling to suggest that he and I meet and have lunch when I came to the city with the corrected galleys. So that's what happened; this morning, I shook the sand off, put on actual clothing with shoes for the first time in two weeks, gathered up my galleys, and took the 10:15 ferry to catch the 11:07 train to meet Dewey Heffernan at the Tre Mafiosi at one o'clock.

The transition from Fire Island to New York is always traumatic, even without Dewey Heffernan. On Fire Island there are no automobiles, no tall buildings, very little noise. I almost never wear shoes there, and certainly not socks. Unless there's something somebody wants to watch on television, we never know the exact time, and couldn't care less. The air is clearer and less humid, and the temperature is usually five to ten degrees cooler than in the city. Last week, Ginger had had to make that awful transition five days in a row

(while worrying unnecessarily about me alone
out here with Mary), but now Mary was gone
(I'd seen no point in describing our nonsexual
encounter to Ginger) and Ginger was in full
residence, and *I* was the one who had to leave
Eden for Mordor.

And Dewey Heffernan. I arrived at the restaurant ten minutes early, planning to have a
drink at the bar while waiting, and he was
already there. Now, I had an excuse for being
early, since I was tied to railroad and ferry
schedules, but for him the restaurant was a
mere five minute walk from the office, so his
presence so early was a baffling but troubling
sign.

So was his *presence*, if you know what I
mean. With Vickie, and earlier with Jack
Rosenfarb, I had always lunched at one of the
banquettes or alcoved tables around the edges
of the room, but this time the maitre d' led
me to a tiny table in the middle of the place,
at which sat something that might have been
Raskolnikov, if it had had any gumption.

This was Dewey Heffernan. When he stood
up, as he did at my arrival, smiling and bob-
bing his head and extending his skinny pale
hand to be shaken, he proved to be a long
drink of water, probably six-four. He was very
thin and bony, and the salesman who'd sold
him that sport jacket must have some sense of
humor. It was a large yellow thing of giant
checks, like what Bob Hope used to wear when
playing in Damon Runyon stories, and it made

Dewey Heffernan look as though he were wearing a taxicab. Somewhere in there were a white shirt and tan tie, possibly belonging to the driver.

Then there's the Dewey Heffernan head. A very high and shiny ivory forehead was surrounded by spikes and thistles of rough black horsehair. A scraggly beard and moustache with intermittent white skin in it looked like the symptom of some awful dermatological disorder. Between these two unfortunate examples of hair-growth was a retroussé nose with nostrils that looked out at the world rather than demurely down at his lip, a broad mouth full of big square teeth, and spaniel eyes that blinked and stared and beheld the variety of the world with unflagging wonder. "You must be Tom Diskant!" said this wonder, happy as a fresh-hatched cuckoo, as the maitre d' pulled out my chair.

"If I must, I must," I said fatalistically, accepted his overly energetic handshake, and took the seat the maitre d' punched into the back of my knees. "Sorry I'm early." I put the galleys package to one side on the table.

Dewey dropped into his chair. "Boy, I know what you mean! I was too excited to hang around the office!"

"Would you gentlemen care for something from the bar?"

"Nah," Dewey said. "Gee, Tom, I— Wait a minute; do you want a drink or something?"

"Maybe so," I said casually. "Bourbon and

soda." (There's something about meeting a new editor that drives me to that particular drink.)

"I guess I'll try one of those, too," Dewey said, grinning at the maitre d', who gave him the old fish-eye and stalked off.

Dewey's happy face zeroed in on me again. "Gee, Tom," he said, "I'm really happy about this. When Miss Douglas handed the file over, she said you were a little worried, maybe the new editor wouldn't be as enthusiastic as she was, but gosh, Tom, I want you to know I think *The Christmas Book* is just great! I mean it, it's fabulous!"

"Thank you," I said modestly.

"See, I have a lot of ideas about publishing," he said, shoving his silverware and display plate out of the way so he could lean his forearms on the table. "New ideas to shake up the whole industry!"

"Ah."

"And this book of yours, Tom, this book of yours fits right into what I'm thinking about."

That was depressing. I looked politely interested.

"Pictures," he said. "Color. Youth appeal. You see what I mean?"

"Yes, I do," I said.

"We've got to attract that youth audience, Tom," he told me. "*Those* are the readers of the *future*!"

"Undoubtedly true."

"They *see* things differently, Tom! They're

used to, they're used to, *video* screens. Display! Computer programs! Rock and roll!''

"Ah hah."

"If we want youth to be interested in *us*, Tom," he said, leaning close over his forearms, eyes and nostrils staring impassionedly at me, "*we* have to be interested in what interests *youth*."

"Interesting," I said, as our waiter brought our drinks.

Dewey lifted his. "To a long association, Tom!"

"Mmm," I said.

We drank, he putting away close to half his bourbon and soda at once, then grinning and nodding and gesturing with the glass as he said, "Nice!"

I thought: He has never tasted bourbon before. "Dewey," I said, "if we're going to get to know one another, maybe you could tell me a little about yourself."

"Oh, sure," he said. "See, I've always been interested in books, you know."

But he was interrupted at that point by the waiter, bringing us our menus and wishing to tell us today's specials. He did so in a sepulchral tone, as though reporting a list of towns destroyed by the Italian earthquake, during which the happy Dewey polished off his drink. When the funeral march of specials was done, the waiter picked Dewey's glass out of his fingers and said, "Would you care for another, sir?"

"Yeah, sure! Tom?"

"I'll nurse this one," I said.

The waiter went away, and Dewey said, "Let's see. Where was I?"

"Interested in books."

"Right. So naturally I was an American Lit major. Northwestern. I got my Master's in June and came straight to New York!"

I stared at him. I couldn't think of a single thing to say.

"I have a cousin at Random House," this Master went on, "but there weren't any openings there—"

Smart cousin.

"—but he has a good friend on the board at Solenex, so he—"

"Solenex?"

"That's the company that owns Craig, Harry & Bourke."

"Oh," I said. I had vaguely known that Craig, like most of the other New York publishing companies, was no longer an actual independent publisher but was a subsidiary of some conglomerate somewhere, but the fact had never seemed to matter very much. Not till now.

"Anyway," Dewey said, "this fellow at Solenex called somebody at Craig, Harry & Bourke, and the next thing I knew, I was an editor!"

This is not happening, I thought. And yet it was. The waiter brought Dewey's new drink and I said, "On second thought, I believe I will have another."

The waiter gave me a dirty look and went away, and Dewey said, "Of course, this is still a trial period for me."

"For all of us," I said.

"Eh?"

"Nothing. Never mind. Tell me more."

He gulped half a drink. "For right now, of course," he said, "I'm not generating any of my own projects, but that will come. What I've got on my plate so far is three books from Miss Douglas, and some war books a man named Scunthorpe had."

"The fellow who died."

"Oh, is that what happened to him?" *Glugg* went more bourbon into the Heffernan maw. "Anyway, what's so exciting about *your* book is how it fits in so perfectly with what I want to do *anyway*!"

"That is nice."

"See," he said, gesturing widely, "I want to do *adult* books, but with the *zing* and *zip* of juveniles!"

"Oh?"

"Science fiction!" He brought his unsteady hands close together over the table, palms down and cupped slightly, as though holding down a soccer ball. "Books that just, just—*fly* out at you!" And his hands flew up and out and away, just missing the waiter with my new drink. "Pop-ups!" Dewey went on, all oblivious, staring madly at me. "You know what I mean? They put 'em in *kids'* books! Why not grown-up books?"

"Pop-ups in grown-up books," I said.

The waiter said, "Would you care to order?"

Dewey drained his drink. "Yeah!" he said, but to me, not the waiter. "Start with science fiction, just to get the idea across, see? You turn the page, and the *planet* comes up, or the *spaceship* comes up!"

Or the lunch, I thought.

The waiter said, "Are you ready to order, gentlemen?"

"But it wouldn't," Dewey said, "it wouldn't, it wouldn't have to *stop* there! All kinds of books. *War* books, historicals! You turn the page, and there's the cavalry right there, comes right up!"

"And there's always pornography," I suggested.

Dewey blinked owlishly at me, stymied. The waiter said, "*Would* you like to order now?"

"Yes," I said firmly. "I'll have the sole *Veronique.*"

"And to begin?"

"The endive salad."

"Thank you." He turned to Dewey. "Sir?"

Dewey frowned massively, looking utterly helpless. "I don't know, I—" He stared at the closed menu beside him, then looked at me. "What was that you said?"

"Sole *Veronique.*"

"Okay." Dewey nodded to the waiter as he pointed at me. "That's what I'll have."

"And to begin?"

"Begin?" said Dewey.

"The other gentleman is having the endive salad."

"Oh. Okay. I'll have that, too. Oh, and another one of these drink things."

"Yes, sir."

The waiter left. Dewey rubbed a knuckly hand over his mouth, frowning at his place. A busboy removed the display plates, which startled Dewey; he jumped slightly, then stared after the busboy. I said, "What does Wilson have to say about *The Christmas Book*, do you know?"

He considered that. "Who?"

"Robert Wilson. The managing editor, or whatever his title is. The man in charge."

"Oh. I haven't met him. Actually, I haven't met many people yet. It's the slow season, the summer."

"Yes."

"I suppose it'll pick up in September." He sounded a bit wistful.

"Yes, it probably will."

Conversation lagged until his next drink was brought; after one slug, he grinned at me and said, "Let's talk about the book."

"Good," I said. "Let's."

"It isn't too late to add stuff," he said. "I asked around specifically on that, and we still have time."

"The book's pretty full, Dewey," I said.

"Well, we could take some stuff out," he

said. "There's some kinda downers in there, all that Death Row stuff and all."

"Norman Mailer won't give the money back," I said.

He didn't understand me. "What?"

"I'm pretty sure Truman Capote won't either."

"Money?"

"The publisher has *paid* for all those things, Dewey," I explained. "I think the company would be upset if they paid for things and then we didn't use them."

"Oh," he said. "Well, what about the real old stuff? Old paintings and things."

"What did you want to replace them with, Dewey?" Our endive salads arrived, but I paid no attention. I was visualizing Santa Clauses, popping-up.

But what Dewey said was, *"Heavy Metal."*

"Beg pardon?"

"You know. The cartoonists that work in *Heavy Metal* or *The National Lampoon."*

"Heavy Metal's a magazine," I said, remembering.

"Yeah, sure! It's *youth*, Tom!"

Youth. Anatomically correct sex comic strips; science fiction comic strips in which people's heads are blown off in careful red detail; drug comic strips. In place of all those old paintings and things.

Dewey was saying, "We could get some *great* stuff from those guys, Tom! Korban! Crumb!

Really terrific impact, audience grabbers. Put some *zing* in the book!''

I filled my mouth with endive, to give me time to think. Watching me do so, Dewey did the same. And what I thought was this: This creature cannot actually hurt me, because his ideas are utterly impractical and absurd. We are to have copies of this book in the stores late in October, which means that now, late in July, there isn't time to commission a *Heavy Metal* cartoonist to give us a drawing of Santa Claus fucking a space monkey. So he is merely babbling, and cannot actually *hurt* me at all.

And what I further thought was this: On the other hand, Dewey Heffernan cannot help me in any way. His eagerness for the book adds up to the same thing as some other caretaker editor's indifference, because nobody over at Craig will give this buffoon the time of day. Even if he knew *how* to talk to publicity or sales or production, even if he could find his way to their offices, they would pay him not the slightest bit of attention. What I have been given for an editor this time is a vacuum.

And what I finally thought was this: Since he can neither hurt nor help me, since he is merely a child learning how to use a push-button phone and what you do in a midtown restaurant at lunchtime, since he is merely a trainee learning at my expense—who, if he remembers this lunch at all ten years from now, will look back on it in wincing embarrassment—there's no point getting mad at him, or insulting him, or getting on my high horse. So I swallowed my endive, and took a deep breath, and smiled, and said, "Good salad, huh?"

"Yeah!" he said.

He ordered another bourbon when the sole *Veronique* came. No one mentioned wine, and I chose not to have a third drink. Dewey was very amused about the grapes on his fish. He told me about college days, and about his plans for knocking the publishing world on its ear, and in the course of lunch he became quite drunk. The waiter and I both had to help him figure out the tip and how to sign the credit card slip and all that, and then he would have left the galleys package behind if I hadn't remembered it. He didn't seem to realize he was drunk, but just thought he was having a good time.

I walked him as far as his building, which I felt was good Samaritan enough; when last seen, Dewey was staggering toward the wrong bank of elevators, the galleys package clutched to his chest the way schoolgirls carry their books.

I then took a train, and the 3:50 ferry, and walked to this house where I have removed most of my clothes, and now it's *my* turn to get drunk.

Sunday, July 31st

HOME again. In more ways than one, since I finally have my office back. Though that may not be permanent.

At the moment, Lance has taken Gretchen and Joshua to California for a two-week stay with relatives of his—of theirs, too, come to think of it—in Marin County, north of San Francisco. He'll be back in two weeks, and is supposed to have some sort of alternate living quarters worked out by then, but I must say I've begun to lose faith in Lance's ability to get his life in order.

After its shaky beginning, with Mary and the blessedly-departed Vickie, the month's vacation worked out very well. The kids took care of themselves to an extent that just isn't possible here in the city, and Ginger and I had time to get sort of reacquainted and remember why we'd come together in the first place. I did a lot of work—magazine pieces, and a start on a presentation for a book about the history of greeting cards that Annie thinks maybe she can get Hallmark or somebody to subsidize—and we both got healthier and healthier, and hardly fought at all.

Friday was Ginger's thirty-fourth birthday; the annual trauma. Nobody ever wants to be the age they are, and this was no exception We went to the local restaurant, Le Dock, just the two of us, and splurged on champagne, and Ginger got wistful and misty-eyed toward the end of the evening, saying, "Where are we headed, Tom? Where are we going? What are we doing? Where are we all headed?"

"Ginger," I said, my hand on hers on the table, "why don't we get married?"

She looked at me with such alarm and shock that I thought she might leap to her feet in another instant and flee the table, the restaurant, the island and possibly the country. However, she didn't; instead, she stared wide-eyed at me while I had plenty of time to realize what an insane thing that had been to suggest: What if she'd said yes?

Well, she wasn't going to say yes, that much was clear from the beginning. What she did say, at last, on a rising inflection, was, "Whaa-aatt?"

Did I have to repeat myself? Did I now have to justify my moment's madness? "It just seemed an idea," I said.

She withdrew her hand from mine, closed it around the champagne glass, and shakily drank. Then she frowned at me for a few seconds, frowned at the table, shook her head and said, in a tone of quiet awe, "That was really very *nice*," as though things that were nice came her way so seldom she hardly recognized them. "It was," she said, agreeing with herself, and looked at me again as a pair of large tears grew in her eyes and rolled down her cheeks, glistening in the candlelight. "That was so sweet, Tom," she said, putting her hand back on mine. "I'll never forget that."

I probably never will, either.

It did all end well, however, my gesture accepted for the noble act it was, without my having to stand by it. We weaved our way homeward from the restaurant by the pale light of the just-past-full moon and sat on the rear deck in the silver darkness for nearly an hour, silent, holding hands. I fell asleep for a while, and I think Ginger did, too.

The next day, yesterday, Lance came out in the morning to hamper his children's packing. Kids travel with ridiculous things, and they never seem to mind how many different suitcases and cartons and duffle bags they fill: "You can't *carry* that much," is being said, at any instant in time, by probably several thousand exasperated parents to several thousand uncomprehending children all over America. In this instance, of course, I was all in favor of Gretchen and Joshua taking with them to Marin County every comic book, every soccer ball, every shiny stone and broken scallop shell, every LP record and tattered magazine and half-deck of playing cards and single sneaker and cuddly doll and Incredible Hulk poster they *wanted* to take to Marin County, because otherwise *I* would have to transport all that crap here to New York; which eventually, of course, I did have to do, today.

At the last possible minute yesterday, Gretchen realized there were several thousand other Gretchens (all these kids look the same and most of them have the same half-dozen names, it's like a science-fiction movie) that she *must* say goodbye to, so off she went, so of course they missed that ferry and Lance had a conniption, and pretty soon everybody was yelling at everybody else, except that Ginger and I didn't have any reason to yell at one another and therefore didn't, which even further increased our sense of solidarity.

Lance, in his rage, kept establishing the point that this delay would mean they'd have to take a taxi from Bay Shore directly to Kennedy Airport in order not to miss their plane, rather than take the Long Island Railroad to Jamaica and *then* a cab which he had previously worked out and which would be much less expensive, but it's useless to talk to children about how expensive or cheap things are. They knew Lance was angry, that's as far as their comprehension could go. Gretchen blubbered until the next boat, and was still blubbering as it left to cross the Great South Bay, and for all I know she's still blubbering now, in Marin County.

Profiting by Lance's example, I ordered Bryan and Jennifer to say *their* goodbyes before lunch today and refused to let them out of my sight for the two hours between the end of lunch and the departure of our ferry, when we would be doing our packing anyway. Nevertheless, various troubles and traumas did arise, and this time Ginger and I did have reasons to yell at one another and therefore did, but nobody's bad temper lasted very long because in truth we'd liked the month in that house and were all sorry to be leaving.

The simple life. Why not?

Wednesday, August 10th

DEWEY Heffernan *is* a menace. Fortunately, so far, he's mostly a menace to himself.

He phoned me yesterday, and at first I couldn't figure out what he was talking about. He said, "Tom, we've got a problem here with the bosses."

"We do? What problem?" But what I was thinking was, *What bosses?* Tell me who you're having trouble with, and I'll tell you if it's serious or not.

But Dewey answered the question I'd asked, rather than the one left unspoken. He said, "Well, they're dragging their feet on this idea we talked about at lunch. Now, I have an artist that has to be paid, and Accounting just kicked the voucher back to me, says it isn't *authorized*. Can you imagine?"

"Not yet," I said. "What artist?"

"You know," he said. "The one to replace the Dürer."

Dürer. There was in the book—page 173, as I recalled—an Albrecht Dürer woodcut called "The Adoration of the Magi," which I had chosen partially because in it St. Joseph looks like John Ehrlichman, but also because Dürer didn't have to be *paid*. You don't pay an artist who's been dead since 1528.

But wait a minute; *replace* the Dürer? I said, "What do you mean, replace?"

"Well, I knew you felt strongly about the color stuff," he said, "and Korban agreed he could give me a good page in black-and-white, so the Dürer just seemed the obvious thing to come out. I didn't see any point bothering you with a detail like that, I mean we have so *much* old stuff."

"Korban," I said, reaching out at random for something that might be forced to make sense. "What is a Korban?"

"He's fantastic!" Dewey told me. "He did the most fantastic freaked-out space trip with Santa Claus and the reindeer and this *wild* nun with an Afro and—"

"Dewey," I said.

"—the sled's like a *low*-rider, and—"

"Dewey!"

"—they go— What?"

"*Heavy Metal*," I said, remembering our lunchtime conversation.

"Sure!"

"You want to commission a *Heavy Metal* artist to do a drugged Santa Claus and—"

"It's *done*, Tom! You ought to come into the office, look at it, it's fantastic!"

"I'm sure it is," I said.

"But now I got to get this poor guy paid," Dewey said. "And Accounting's making all this trouble."

I said, "Dewey, are you telling me you went out all on your own and commissioned an illustration for *The Christmas Book*?"

"The one we talked about at—"

"Not me," I said.

"What?" The sound was so baffled, so lost and hopeless, that I knew this was merely another example of Dewey's ignorance and that he hadn't been trying to pull a fast one at all. I don't think Dewey would know a fast one if he fell over it, which he most likely would. "What, Tom?" this innocent asked.

I said, "Dewey, at that lunch I did not agree that we should add the work of a *Heavy Metal* cartoonist to *The Christmas Book*."

"Tom, you did!"

"I did not, I would not, and I will not."

"Tom, I distinctly remember—"

"You do not," I said. "You do not distinctly remember *anything* from that lunch. *I* distinctly remember the lunch, and I remember you talked about pop-up books for adults, and I remember you talked about the *Heavy Metal* artists, and I remember the conversation remained theoretical."

"Tom, you thought it was a good idea!"

"I thought it was a rotten idea. I also thought it was something you couldn't possibly do in July for a book to be published in October, so there was no reason to argue."

"But we *talked* about it!"

"Who else did you talk to?"

"Korban! The artist!"

"Who did you talk to at Craig?"

"Nobody," he said, and for the first time a trace of doubt—or perhaps fear—entered his voice.

I said, "So you just went out, without my approval or any permission from anybody at Craig, and offered some clown— How much did you offer him?"

"Fifteen hundred dollars," he said. Now he was definitely scared.

"Where did you come up with the number?"

"I looked to see what we paid the other artists," he said. "So I offered him the same. Tom, it's a really wonderful—"

"And then you put in two vouchers to Accounting," I said, being deliberately mean, "and they bounced them back at you."

"Two vouchers? No, just one."

"What about my thousand dollars?" I asked him.

"Tom? What are you talking about?"

"Dewey," I said, "you're the editor on this book. Haven't you read the contract? Haven't you read the correspondence? Haven't you talked with *anybody* about this book?"

"There's nobody here to talk to," he said miserably. "Everybody's gone away for August."

"According to the terms of the contract," I told him, "the contributors receive sixty per cent of the advance, and I receive forty per cent. Everybody has been paid and that part of the deal is done and finished with, but if Craig is now going to pay an additional fifteen hundred dollars to a contributor, then they must pay an additional thousand to me."

"But they won't *pay* him, that's the problem!"

"Dewey, I hate to tell you this," I said, "but that isn't the problem. The problem is that you gave an unauthorized assignment to an artist. Did you make the proposal in a letter? On Craig letterhead?"

"Why?"

"Because if Craig refuses to pay," I said, "and I imagine they will refuse to pay, your artist probably has a good lawsuit on his hands."

"A lawsuit?" He did sound more and more like a mountain climber who's just seen the end of the rope fall past.

But I was pitiless. "Against Craig," I said. "But then Craig would naturally recover the money by suing you. Whether I'd sue for my thousand or not I'm not sure at this point."

"Tom, you don't mean that!"

"I don't mean I'm not sure?"

"Tom, listen. If we use the strip in the book, they *have* to pay."

"We will not use the strip in the book."

"I already sent the original to the printer," he said. "I already told him to pull the Dürer."

"Oh, you bastard," I said. "Oh, you baby asshole."

"Tom, we talked about this at *lunch*! We *did*!"

"You call that printer right now, tell him—"

"Tom Tom Tom! *Please*, Tom, you have to be on my side!"

"The hell I do."

"You have to *see* this strip!"

"Not in the book, I don't."

"We have to use it or they won't *pay*!"

"You have to clear it first before you offer money!"

"I talked about it with *you*!"

"I don't disburse Craig's money! I *im*burse Craig's money!" I yelled, inventing new languages in my aggravation.

"Tom, it's only one *page*!"

"In MY BOOK, schmuck!"

There was a little silence, in which we both breathed heavily, and then he said, in a small voice, "Tom, I need your help. You're the only one I can turn to."

Jesus. Now I'm supposed to feel guilty because *he's* a buffoon. I'm supposed to feel guilty because the people nominally in charge left him running the candystore and he's been giving away the candy. I said, "Dewey, let me give you some advice. How well do you know this Koben?"

"Korban," said the small voice. "Not very well."

"All right. The first thing you do, you phone the printer and countermand your first instruction. The Dürer goes in, the—"

"Tom, please! Please!"

"The other goddam thing goes *out*. Now, the second thing you do, there must have been *somebody* in that organization who talked to you when you were hired. Find that person. If he's away on vacation, get somebody to give you the phone number, and call him. Tell him what you've done, say you're sorry, say it was a mistake, throw yourself on his mercy."

"Tom—"

"Third," I insisted, "call the artist, tell him exactly what happened—"

"I'm not sure I know what happened."

"You exceeded your authority," I told him. "Is that clear enough?"

"I didn't know I— I didn't realize—"

"I've got that. Anyway, ask the artist if he can sell the work somewhere else; maybe for the *Heavy Metal* Christmas issue. If he wants, you know, he can still stick you for the fifteen hundred. If you're lucky, maybe you can talk him out of it."

"Tom, if we use it we won't have to—"

"We will not use it."

"You haven't even *seen* it! You're just throwing your weight around because you *can*!"

"Weight? What weight? I can't even keep *you* from fucking around with my book."

"I thought— I thought we *liked* each other!"

"Dewey, Dewey, Dewey," I said, and broke the connection because there really was absolutely nothing more to say, and called Annie. I described the situation to her, and she sighed and said she'd see what she could do, and I said, "The Dürer goes back in the book, Annie."

"Oh, I agree," she said. "It's just how much trouble there is along the way."

Oh, how *much* trouble there is along the way, after all. I am sitting here in my air-conditioned office, away from the August heat and humidity, putting the finishing touches on the presentation for the history of greeting cards, and that total jerk over at Craig is turning *The Christmas Book* into *Zap* Comics!

I do feel sorry for him, in a way. He knows so little about anything that he doesn't even know how much he doesn't know. His employers turned him loose without a thought, figuring the only people he could hurt were the writers, and now he's hurt himself and possibly them. Will they fire him? Am I about to have my *fourth* editor?

It's like one of the plagues of Egypt; a plague of editors. No, that's *worse* than the plagues of Egypt.

Monday, August 15th

THE quick brown fox jumped over the lazy dogs.

It feels strange to be back in this room again, working at this table. Strange and a little scary; I'm not sure I know what it means.

All I know is what happened. Yesterday, Lance brought the kids back from Marin County, happy and bouncing and full of stories about redwood trees and the Pacific Ocean and the strange-looking males of San Francisco. Unfortunately, Lance also brought himself back, and in the middle of the afternoon it became obvious he intended to stay. I said, "Lance, what about the other arrangements you were making?"

"They didn't pan out," he said. "But I've still got some possibilities."

So as soon as I could I cornered Ginger in

the bedroom and said, "Ginger, this has got to stop."

"Well, *I* didn't invite him back," she said. She seemed irritated with both of us.

"He can't take over my office again," I said. "That's all there is to it."

"Well, then, tell him so. *You* tell him."

"I'll be delighted," I said, but when I turned toward the door she cried, "Tom!" I looked back at her: "What?"

"We can't do that! It is his place, too, he still pays rent, he—"

"So do I pay rent! In fact, I *live* here. Does Lance live here?"

"I don't know what you mean."

"I mean, are we just putting Lance up until he finds a new apartment, or has he moved back in?"

"He has *not* moved back in!" This was the most appalling idea she'd heard since my proposal of marriage.

"It sure looks like he has," I said. "And the worst of it is, he's moved into *my* office."

"It can't be much longer, Tom," she said, switching gears, deciding to try to placate me.

"It's already been too long. You know, I could always go work downtown."

"You mean, at Craig? At Annie's?"

"No. The room I used to use as an office is—"

"You mean at *Mary's*?"

"She told me a while ago, if I ever needed an office, the one I used to have is—"

"That *bitch*!"

"Mary isn't pushing me *out* of places to work, Ginger," I said. "If Lance moves into that office tonight, I'll start using my old office tomorrow."

"Go right ahead, then," she said. "I think it's ridiculous to make such a fuss, but if that's what you want to do . . ."

"That's what I want to do," I said, although of course it wasn't at all what I wanted to do. What I wanted to do was force Ginger to kick Lance out, figuring she would certainly do so if the alternative was that I'd be spending every day with Mary.

But somehow it didn't work out. I moved firmly forward, ostentatiously packing up my typewriter and a carton of notes and reference books, and Ginger didn't say a word on the subject. I phoned Mary to ask if the offer was still good, and she said yes, and I said I'd be down this morning, and Ginger stood firm. Lance moved into my office last night, and my office moved out this morning. I left a different message on the answering machine up there, directing callers to reach me down here, and brought everything I needed down in a cab.

Like the room uptown, this one is simply the smallest bedroom in the apartment, similarly with a view of an airshaft. The few times I'd looked in the doorway here over the last year or so my old table and chair and waste-basket were still in place, but the room had become increasingly filled with stored cartons or mounds of off-season or outgrown clothing. Mary has always had a small portable inconvenient darkroom in our bathroom (how nice it has been to start the days without those acrid smells or that cumbersome boxy machinery in the way), and would hang her prints to dry on a cord stretched over the tub, but a few months ago a clothesline appeared in my ex-office, extending from a nail over the door to a nail over the window, and from it has dangled a gallery of her game attempts at art or commerce or at least legibility: winos asleep in doorways, close-ups of snowy fire escapes, a tiny girl studying a mosquito bite.

But this morning the clothesline was gone, and so were the cartons and the clothing. The room was bare and clean, exactly as I'd left it eighteen months ago. Mary had gone out to the Picture Collection at the Mid-Manhattan Library on a research job, and had left a note: "Won't be back till late. Help yourself in the kitchen."

I have helped myself in the kitchen. I have wandered around the apartment, looking into the kids' rooms and into Mary's room while memories have stirred, and I have felt increasingly uneasy. For some reason, the troubles we had, the bad times, the abrasions when we were throwing each other off like heavy colds after taking an antibiotic, all those moments and feelings have faded away like invisible ink. Even the chemical stink bleeding into the bedroom through the closed bathroom door no longer irritates. All I can find here now, out of the past, is our sporadic happiness.

I'm beginning to believe Thomas Wolfe had it wrong: it isn't that you can't go home again, it's that you shouldn't.

Wednesday, August 17th

WHAT really pisses me off is that even *Annie* thinks I'm wrong. She won't say so, but I can tell from the tone of her voice.

I am talking about Dewey Heffernan and Craig and the *Heavy Metal* artist named Korban. It turns out that Korban, despite the juvenile content of his material, is not a Dewey-style eager amateur but a professional illustrator with an agent and an attorney and probably an accountant and a broker and a personal hitman as well. They are referred to by Annie generically—and admiringly—as "Korban's people," and their attitude is simple and straightforward. Their man was commissioned to do a certain piece of work for a certain agreed-on sum; he did the piece of work, and he is now to be paid the agreed-on sum. There are no alternatives, there is no other way to look at the thing.

As for the *thing*, the comic strip, there's no way to look at that at all. At Annie's insistence, I agreed last Friday at least to gaze upon the result of Mister Korban's inspiration and labors, with as open a mind—and eyes—as possible, so Friday afternoon somebody from Craig messengered a Xerox of the thing to my office—uptown, before I came down here to Mary's—and I taped it to the wall over the desk and spent some time brooding at it.

At first I almost thought, what the hell, why not. The thing is, I've been getting into high gear with this greeting card history—I've got cards and photos of cards and doggerel verses from cards all *over* this room now, taped to the walls and the back of the door, stacked on the radiator cover, spreading out over the floor like pink and gold ivy—and Korban's irreverence was initially an almost pleasant respite from the saccharine overdose I've been taking. Also, his draftsmanship is excellent, and he pays careful attention to detail; the elbows are as meticulously rendered as the pudendae.

However. I spent last weekend with my kids, and then with the trauma of Lance's return, and then with the move downtown, by the end of which I had come to the conclusion that maybe it wasn't so bad after all, but when I saw it again on Monday—while taping it up, along with everything else, in this new/old office—I realized it was impossible, so I phoned Annie and said so. "Whatever you want," she said, dubiously.

What's wrong with Korban's work—apart from the thuggish crudity of the mind behind it—is what tends to be wrong with a lot of things directed at young people; it's nihilistic for fun. In a nervous effort to be knowing before they know anything, not to be taken in, a lot of kids throw out the sentiment with the sentimentality and are left with nothing but surface. Then they try to replace what they've lost by being sentimental about themselves. (None of this is new, of course; remember "Teen Angel"?)

But the caustic harshness still such a strong element in this tripe is a leftover from the anti-war, pro-drug sixties, and is nastily inappropriate in the me-first eighties. It is true that some of the contributors to *The Christmas Book* are cynical about Christmas, but it's an earned cynicism. Korban may have earned his fifteen hundred dollars, but he hasn't earned his attitudes, and I won't have his work in the book.

Which is where the problem comes in, and why it's now all *my* fault. It has been a week since Dewey first lobbed this mortar shell onto my desk and I went running with it to Annie, and this is the way it has been resolved. Craig will pay Korban his fifteen hundred, because Craig has no choice in the matter. I refuse to run Korban's work—Dürer is back in, where he belongs—so Craig will not pay me my forty per cent. And whereas the powers at Craig ought to be angry at Dewey for placing them in a position where they have to throw away fifteen hundred dollars, it turns out they're angry at *me* because it's my *refusal* that makes the fifteen hundred a waste.

To one extent or another, everybody—even Annie and Ginger—has assumed the same attitude about this as Dewey; it's only one page, why make a fuss? Until now, I hadn't realized that such a question could even exist. So at the end not only is Dewey not fired, he's the wronged one, and is still my editor, and *he's* mad at me for betraying him!

I have now turned my back on *The Christmas Book*, having given it the supreme sacrifice. No, not the thousand bucks, but the fragile good will that had existed between me and my publisher. I am keeping Korban's craftsmanlike slop on my wall amid the greeting cards, to remind me that the unforeseen is *always* what goes wrong, and I am hoping that Annie will sell Hallmark, and Hallmark will sell some other publishing house, and in that publishing house I shall at last find an ally who won't quit, get pregnant, or enter second childhood before leaving the first.

Friday, August 19th

YESTERDAY was Gretchen's ninth birthday, and when I was leaving the office to go up-town Mary handed me a shopping bag containing two gift-wrapped packages, saying, "Would you give these to Gretchen with my love?"

"Hey, that's nice," I said. "You didn't have to do that."

"I wanted to."

"Okay. Well, I—"

"Tom," she said. "Could we talk for a minute?"

I looked at her warily. I've been working down here all week now, and so far Mary had not tried to make any capital out of the situation. She hadn't pushed domesticity, she hadn't created conversations out of the children's emotional needs, and—best of all—she had given me no more examples of the world engaging in foreplay with her. Was all that about to change?

Not exactly. We sat together in the living room, and she astounded me completely by saying, "I want to talk to you about Gretchen."

"Gretchen!"

"She's a very nice girl," Mary said.

"Sure she is."

"She's three years younger than Jennifer, so naturally she isn't as advanced, but she's very bright and sweet, and she has a very good artistic eye."

What on Earth was this about? I snuck a look at my watch, and was about to say something about not wanting to be late for the kid's birthday party, when Mary said, "I don't think you have the slightest idea what you're doing to that child."

"Doing—I'm not doing *anything* to that child."

"You're rejecting her," Mary said.

"Oh, for Pete's— In the first place," I said, "I'm not rejecting her at all, I was just this minute thinking I didn't want to be late for her birthday party. And in the second place, I get all the Gretchen commercials I need from Ginger, so don't *you* start."

Mary smiled, in that infuriating way she has. "I didn't think Ginger would sit by and take it quietly," she said.

"Take what quietly?" I demanded, then hurried on, saying, "There's nothing to take!"

"When you and I separated," she said, "you had what seemed to you good reasons."

"They were good reasons."

"Whether they were or not," she said, "you never intended to leave the children."

"I didn't lea— Well, I did, but— Of course not."

"You've been very good with them, Tom," she assured me. "You're around them as much as you can, you care about them, you let them see you love them and want the best for them."

"Thank you," I said.

"Bryan and Joshua get along wonderfully well," she said, "and that makes it easier for you, you can treat them almost as twins, do things together with both of them, take them to that baseball game."

"I enjoyed it."

"Of course you did. But with Jennifer and Gretchen it's harder. There's three years between them, they aren't natural pals, and of course a girl's relationship with her father is more complicated than a boy's anyway."

"I don't get the point," I said.

"Sometimes," she said, "you're not sure the children really understand you didn't mean to leave *them* when you left *me*. So you try too hard sometimes."

"I know I do. It's the Divorced Daddy Syndrome, everybody knows about that."

"One of the ways," she said, "that you assure Jennifer you still love her is to assure everybody you don't love Gretchen."

"That's ridiculous," I said. "*Love* Gretchen? What has that got to do with anything?"

"You're in the role of father there," she said. "You're living with her mother, you're the one who's there all the time."

"Lance is around," I said bitterly. "Don't worry about him, he's around."

"But that's only recently. For a year and a half, you've been more Gretchen's father than Lance, and you've been very cold to her all that time. And it isn't necessary, Tom. Gretchen's a nice little girl, and Jennifer won't mind if you treat her kindly."

I wanted to defend myself, but was Mary wrong? Generally, I felt Gretchen was a little pest, a minor annoyance, something I had to put up with if I was going to live with Ginger. Was that being unfair? I said, "Mary, I don't know if you're right or not. Maybe you are, but maybe the truth is Gretchen really isn't very likable. Maybe there's a little bit of both there; I want Jennifer to know I prefer her, and one of the reasons I prefer her is that she's a nicer kid."

"Think about it," Mary said. "All right?"

"Do I have much choice?"

Mary laughed, and patted my arm, and released me then, and on I went to the birthday party; a perfect time and place to brood about whether I was being fair to the birthday girl. My two kids weren't there, only Joshua and Gretchen and four of Gretchen's friends from school and Ginger and Lance (of course) and me. And while trying to think about my relationship with Gretchen—the *existence* of such a thing, never mind its quality, was still astounding to me—I became aware that I was the outsider at this party.

Hey, wait a minute; I hadn't known it was going to be like that. I live here, don't I? Ginger and I are the basic family unit here, plus her kids, right? But all of a sudden we're at Gretchen's birthday party, and the guest list includes her father, her mother, her brother, her friends from school, and some man.

Me.

This made me resentful and edgy, and got in the way of my efforts to study Gretchen calmly and dispassionately, to see if she was a more likable human being than I'd thought. So I came at the problem from a different direction, observing Gretchen's friends to see what they were like, and what my attitude toward them was, and suddenly I realized they were the *same* as Gretchen! And the way in which they were the same, of course, was that they were equally immature, squealing and silly and fluctuating crazily between ridiculous enthusiasm and absurd despair; acting, in other words, their age.

That was a point neither Mary nor I had considered, the fact that Gretchen is, in this postnuclear family, the youngest of four children, still going through phases the other kids have successfully grown out of. It was her babyishness, more than anything else, that had made it possible for me to reject her.

There; I've said it. Reject her. Mary was right, as I gloomily realized while sitting there as the fifth wheel at Gretchen's party, pistachio chocolate-chip ice cream turning to ashes in my mouth. Gretchen was neither better nor worse than any other kid. I had without realizing it tried her and found her guilty of two great crimes: of being the youngest child, and of not being mine.

Various complaints that Ginger had made over the months returned to me, concerning my attitude toward Gretchen, and all at once I saw them in a new light. I *had* dismissed the kid, been cold to her, expressed my impatience around her.

Her drawings for *The Christmas Book.* I now saw—if I was honest, I now could see—that the idea of a child's drawing, one original well-done child's drawing on the subject of Christmas, would have been an excellent addition to the book, blending in very well with the theme. What if *Jennifer* were the one with an artistic bent, what if she had come forward with a contribution for the book, would I have dismissed the idea out of hand?

However, in my defense, I would also point out that I have not included any of Mary's photographs. *The Christmas Book* is a professional piece of work, not an amateur gathering of family and friends.

On the *other* other hand, Mary never volunteered (being a grown-up, and therefore aware of the ground rules) and Jennifer does not have an artistic vocation, so with neither of them did the question have to be faced. Gretchen, too young to understand the difference between my work and her play, offered me an opportunity to rethink *The Christmas Book* just slightly, and I snubbed her, which was not only mean, but also unprofessional.

The birthday party went on. Amid the laughter and the giggling and general good cheer, I became gloomier and gloomier, guiltier and guiltier, more and more depressed. I began to feel like the strange little creature in the corner of an Edward Gorey drawing; the party going on, and the dark monster skulking behind the drapes.

Later last night I asked Ginger, "Where are all those Christmas drawings Gretchen did?"

She looked at me in some surprise. "Why?"

"I wanted to look at them again."

"She threw them away."

"All of them? Are you sure?"

"When you made it clear you didn't want them, what else would she do?"

"Okay," I said. I was thinking, *It's too late anyway.* I was thinking, *After the stink I made about Dewey Heffernan and Korban, I'm not sure I have the nerve to drag in some kid's drawing at the last second, even if there's still time.* I was thinking, *If I ask her to draw another one, I'll just get her hopes up, and then something will go wrong (because something always does), and that'll be worse.* "Doesn't matter," I said, but this morning I went through the boxes of stuff from *The Christmas Book* piled in Lance's room—I don't think of it as my office any more—and then I took a quick look in Gretchen's room (she'd gone off to school), and when I came down here to work I did some more searching, but without finding anything. She really did throw them all away.

I'm glad I let her intercept the football that time. Of course, the one nice thing I ever did for the kid she doesn't know about, and it would be spoiled if she did.

Shit.

Friday, August 26th

ON this date in 1920, the Nineteenth Amendment gave women the vote. On this date in this year, Lance moved out of my uptown office.

Ginger does not like my working at Mary's place one little bit, an attitude she kept very quiet about last week, when I first came down here, but this week she began to agitate. On Monday she said it was "silly" for me to spend my days downtown when Lance was always at work all day long anyway and I could work perfectly well at "home," and I said I needed an office that was my office twenty-four hours a day, so I could leave work-in-progress scattered about.

On Tuesday she called nine times. Mary was out most of the day, so I was the one who had to answer the phone each time, and the calls were never *about* anything, which finally teed me off. "I am *working* here, Ginger," I said. "I am not seducing Mary, and I am not being seduced by Mary, I am working. Except when I have to keep answering the damn phone." She said, "There's no *reason* for you to be there." I said, "The reason is called Lance."

On Wednesday Lance called to say Ginger was phoning *him* every half hour to ask what progress he was making in finding a new place to live; so my original intent was at last beginning to be realized. Lance, with that wistful sound he gets in his voice a lot these days, said, "I didn't know there was such urgency, Tom. I thought you were all right." I said, "There *was* such urgency, Lance, as I damn well tried to make clear, but you out-waited me, so now I'm perfectly happy spending my days at Mary's place, and Ginger's beginning to realize it's *your* fault."

On Thursday, yesterday, at the breakfast table, Ginger pointed a piece of bacon at Lance and said, "I don't want you still here after the first of the month, Lance, I really don't. This has gone on long enough." Lance looked sober and capable, firming his shoulders as he said, "I'm working on it, Ginger, I definitely am." And last night he came home to announce that he had *made* alternate plans, and would be leaving almost immediately.

Which was this morning. We took a cab together, Lance and I and many of his cartons and suitcases. I got out of the cab at 17th Street and he continued on down to Greenwich Street, where he will be—until something else comes along—sharing an apartment with a co-worker named Bradford, who happens to be a manic militant faggot. I have met Bradford a few times, and I do not envy Lance.

Bradford shaves his head but has grown a thick drooping western-style moustache, and he lives a life of signals and symbols. Whenever he's not at work, he wears a black leather bomber jacket and faded blue jeans, which is a virtual uniform for Village queens of a specific type. The bunch of keys dangling from a belt loop and the red bandanna fluttering from a hip pocket describe to the cognoscenti his sexual preferences, about which I want to know as little as possible. They would not include Lance, but even so, Bradford agreed to share his "space" for a while only on condition that Lance realize he, Bradford, frequently made "friends" in the outer world who would return with him for fun and frolic; behind the closed door of a separate bedroom, but even so. Lance has agreed not to remark upon anything that might emerge from that bedroom of a morning, and not to spread any tales around the workplace.

Ginger must have been leaning on Lance really *hard*, if life with Bradford seems the better alternative.

And Ginger isn't even getting what she wanted from it, at least not right away. Last night we had a *huge* row over the fact that I have no intention of moving the office back uptown. "I am in the very middle of assembling *Happy Happy Happy*," I explained several times, that being the working title of the greeting card book. "I not only have things piled up all over that room, taped to the walls, stacked here and there and everywhere, but each pile and each individual thing is where it is for a *reason*. I am assembling sample chapters and an outline of the book, and it would cost me *days* of work to tear that office apart, carry everything up here, and start all over."

"Then do it," she said.

"No," I said.

She is not speaking to me at the moment, which means maybe I can get some work done.

Friday, September 2nd

I hate Dewey Heffernan. He's not only an idiot, he's a nasty idiot.

In the three weeks I've been working downtown, I've left a message on the uptown answering machine, giving this phone number down here and saying this is where I'll be during working hours. Everybody *else* wanting to reach me has managed to work out the intricacies of that message and dial the new number and talk to me—some, by the way, congratulating me on "seeing through" Ginger and returning at last to Mary, which leads to a great deal of embarrassment all around—but could Dewey Heffernan accomplish that great feat? For years I have heard the expression, "He couldn't find his ass with both hands," and thought it hyperbole, but now I

have met someone who couldn't find his ass
with both hands *tied behind him.*

Around six last night I returned to the uptown apartment to find a message on the machine from Dewey: "Give me a call as soon as
you can, Tom. You're being sued." Well, of
course, at that hour everybody was gone from
the Craig, Harry & Bourke offices, so I had a
night to think about that message before I
finally managed to reach Dewey at ten-thirty
this morning. "Sued?" I said. "What have you
done now, Dewey?"

"Gee, Tom," he said, all innocence (which I
no longer trust), "why act like *that*? Gee whiz,
I wasn't the one who made all that trouble."

There are statements so outrageous there's
no response possible at all. Besides, I was
more interested in today's shitstorm than yesterday's. "Tell me about this suit," I said.

"We were served yesterday," he told me.
"They're going to serve you, too, but I guess
they can't find you. You sure are tough to
track down, Tom."

"Who are 'they,' Dewey, and what is the
subject of the lawsuit?"

"Wait a minute, I've got it here somewhere,
I'll just. . . . Hold on, I'm. . . . I know it's. . . ."

There followed a period of sound effects:
rustlings and scuttlings, very like mice in a
wall. This was followed by a brief silence, and
then Dewey, sounding a bit out of breath,
came back on the line, saying, "I'll have to
call you back, Tom," and he hung up.

"Wait!" I said, but of course it was too late.

So *I* called *him* back, and when I got through to him I said, "Since, Dewey, I know you would call me at the other number and leave a message on the machine, why don't I tell you this phone number *here* and save some time?"

"I just found it," he said.

"The phone number?"

"His name is— What?"

"Whose name?"

"The man who's suing you. He's Harold Muddnyfe of Muscatine, Iowa, and he's suing on behalf of his wife Maureen."

"And what am I supposed to have done to Maureen Muddnyfe?"

"Stolen her idea for *The Christmas Book*."

"WHAT?"

"The suit says it was her idea, and she was in correspondence with many of the same people you approached, and you stole her idea and she wants all royalties plus punitive damages."

"Jesus H. Christ!"

"The reason it's the husband doing it is because his wife is in an iron lung."

"Oh, I don't believe this."

"She's been confined to this iron lung for the last twelve years, so all she can do is read, so she's written a lot of letters to writers over the years, she's been in correspondence with all these people, and three years ago she got her idea for a modern book about Christmas,

with things written especially for it by all her
favorite writers, the book to be called *Joy to
the—*"

"Tacky."

"—*World*, and she wrote to a bunch of writers, and they all told her it was a great idea."

"Sure they did," I said. "Of course they did.
The woman's in an iron lung in Muscatel,
Iowa—"

"Musca*tine*."

"Who's going to rain on her parade? Did
she ever approach any publishers?"

"Yes."

"Who?"

Dewey coughed. "Well, us, for one."

"Oh, that's just—" I said, and the doorbell
rang, the upstairs doorbell. "Don't go away,
Dewey," I said. "Do not, under pain of death,
go away." I put the phone down and ran to
the front door and opened it, and standing in
the hall was a woebegone man with a big
nose and a tan raincoat and a folded packet of
papers. He said, "Thomas Diskant?"

"Yes?"

"Here," he said, and gave me the papers.

"What's this?"

"You have been served in a civil suit," the
man said, and walked away.

Son of a bitch! Slamming the door, I ran
back to the phone to find that Dewey—astonish-
ingly enough—had not gone away. "I've just
been served," I said, fumbling to open the

packet and talk on the phone at the same time.

"I knew they'd probably find you," Dewey said, with what sounded suspiciously like satisfaction.

I said, "Is there correspondence between Craig and this Mudsill woman?"

"Muddnyfe."

"Yes, here it is," I said, reading the indictment against me. "Muddnyfe. She has correspondence from Craig?"

"Yes. I've got a copy of the carbon. It just says thank you for your letter, it's an interesting idea, if you do the book we'll be happy to consider it."

The standard brush-off. "What's the date?"

"Well, it's two and a half years ago."

"So it's prior to me and she can prove access. This is terrific. Who signed the letter?"

"Well, it's kind of unreadable," Dewey said. "Nobody seems to know who it is, and the initials on the lower left are all smudged."

"Is there a job title under the unreadable signature?"

"Associate editor."

A slush-pile reader. A recent college graduate, or maybe somebody's wife or boyfriend, long out of that job. There's nobody to say what happened to Maureen Muddnyfe's query letter once it arrived at the Craig, Harry & Bourke offices, no one to swear that it wasn't shown to me (already a Craig author, leave us not forget), no one to state that he or she was

the only person connected with Craig, Harry
& Bourke who read or saw or had any knowledge of that letter. "I think, Dewey," I said, "I
think I ought to call my lawyer."

"Listen, Tom? Can I ask a question?"

"Sure."

"*Did* you?"

"Did I what?"

"Get the idea from this letter."

"Someday, Dewey," I said, "I shall unscrew
your head and bowl with it." I hung up on his
flabbergasted silence—gee whiz, what was old
Tom mad at *now*?—and phoned my attorney,
Morris Morrison, who had taken today off because it was the start of the Labor Day weekend.

Labor Day. *Another* damn holiday. This one
was dreamed up by the Knights of Labor, a
kind of nineteenth century American Wobblies,
a secret society founded in 1869 and dedi-
cated to organizing all workers, skilled and
unskilled, clerical and professional, and even
including small businessmen, into one huge
union. By 1880 they'd come out of the closet
and had started attracting a lot of member-
ship; almost a million by 1886. However, they
were a little too radical for their time, and
believed rather too enthusiastically in con-
frontational strikes. Also, the AFL and other
craft unions were coming along and didn't
want to give up their autonomy to be in this
huge amorphous organization. The result was,
by 1890 the Knights had been unhorsed, never

to return, and by now they're just about completely forgotten.

Except for Labor Day. It was their invention. They chose the date, the first Monday in September, and on that date in 1882, 1883 and 1884 they paraded in New York, demanding a holiday for the workingman (as though the goddam workingman doesn't have enough holidays as it is; but you know what they meant). Every other labor organization joined the effort, and in 1887 Oregon became the first state to make the first Monday in September a holiday devoted to big-L Labor. New York and New Jersey and Colorado (with all those miners to pacify) soon followed, and in 1894 (after the Knights were already kaput) Congress made the affair national. So the Knights of Labor finally accomplished, after heroic effort, just one thing: a day off.

Well, but it's a lot more than one day off by now, isn't it? It's a *looooonnnnng* weekend, with people taking off Friday and probably Tuesday as well.

Oh, my God, I just looked at the calendar, and Rosh Hashanah starts next Thursday! And then Yom Kippur after that. Next Wednesday is the only day in the foreseeable future when I will be able, if I am very very lucky, to talk with my attorney.

If Dewey had only phoned me *here* yesterday. . . .

If Dewey. Is there any point in a sentence that starts, "If Dewey . . ."?

~~~~~~~~~~~~~~~

Monday, September 19th

I'VE been talking to this typewriter less because I've been talking to Mary more. (She's out at the library, and I'm waiting for Annie to call back re Hallmark and the greeting card book.)

At first, I was extremely cautious about talking to Mary, not wanting to sit through any more verbal sex scenes, but they seem suddenly to have stopped. There hasn't been one in the five weeks since I moved my office back here, a change I try not to look at too closely. There has certainly been nothing sexual between Mary and *me* in these five weeks, and yet the other stuff has stopped. All right, it has stopped; I avoid asking why. I merely accept with gratitude the opportunity to talk with Mary again.

In the old days, she and I would discuss the

projects I was working on, the editors I was dealing with, all the nuts and bolts of this endless extrusion of words, and her manner back then was unfailingly calm and encouraging and receptive. It was *so* unfailingly all those things, in fact, that I gradually came to the conclusion I was boring her. Ginger takes a much more emotional part in my day-to-day business affairs, being angry or excited or fearful or expectant on my account, so there's never any question as to whether she really means it. Up till now, I've much preferred Ginger's style to Mary's.

The problem now is, Ginger's emotionalism is precisely the wrong reaction to this lawsuit mess. If I mention it at all to her, she just gets mad (as I did at first), accuses the Muddnyfes of being frauds and conmen, and demands variously that I countersue, that I have nothing to do with the matter, that I write a strongly-worded letter to PEN insisting they take my side in the case, that I sue Craig for letting the situation develop, that I phone Harold Muddnyfe direct and give him a piece of my mind, that I write strongly-worded letters to all the contributors of *The Christmas Book* demanding their moral, emotional *and financial* support, and other similarly helpful suggestions. If I seem less than totally enthusiastic about any of these windmill-chargings, Ginger gets mad at *me*, accuses me of knuckling under, assures me I have a secret urge to fail which is very common among white males of my age and background, informs me I have no backbone, lets me know that I'm afraid of publishers in general and Craig, Harry & Bourke in particular, says I might as well get a job somewhere because I'll clearly never make a living as a freelance, and in other such ways improves the shining hour. So I tend not to bring the subject up.

Mary's calm, on the other hand, has never been more useful. Her assumption (which I now agree with) is that the Muddnyfes are sincere but naive, and that they have merely misunderstood the situation. What good that does me, and whether they will ever smarten up, I do not know, but at least it's comforting to believe that I'm not the object of a conspiracy nor in the grip of a gang of knowing clever confidence men.

It's also comforting to be able to turn to Mary after I've had a conversation with either Dewey (my sole remaining contact at Craig), or with my attorney, Morris, who assures me this case will take "*years* to resolve, Tom, *years*. A fascinating case." You do not want to hear your attorney tell you you have a fascinating case.

No matter what happens, even if I am totally vindicated (as I damn well ought to be), this thing is going to cost me, starting with Morris's fee and the loss of my own time. Craig's attorneys went to court last week to try for a summary dismissal on the basis of the Muddnyfes' action being "frivolous and without merit," but the judge denied the motion, saying a trial would best determine whether the suit had no merit. (Apparently he too thinks it's a fascinating case.)

Now Craig's attorneys are initiating a countersuit, declaring the Muddnyfes' action to be a deliberate "nuisance suit," of a kind fairly common in publishing (apparently, there are a lot of creeps out there who figure it doesn't cost that much to sue, and maybe a big publisher will give them a few thousand bucks to go away and not cause too much trouble), but Morris thinks the Muddnyfes' obvious sincerity and unimpeachable background doom that effort. After all, how much crime or moral turpitude is possible to a woman confined to an iron lung? Nevertheless, Craig and I are contractually lashed together in this enterprise, so I am listed as a party in the countersuit, which *I* think a jury in the main suit (if it ever comes to trial) is likely to hold against me.

Then there are the Muddnyfe attorneys. They have one in Iowa, whose competence, according to Morris, doesn't extend much beyond the drawing up of farmers' wills, but they have a New York attorney as well, since this suit will be tried under the laws of New York State, and their New York attorney is in *Elmira*! What do they know of big-city life, out there in Iowa, of the difference between New York, New York and Elmira, New York, which are just as close together as anything

on the Rand McNally map? And what do they
know of the publishing world in Elmira? Nothing. (Apparently, the Elmira attorney and the
Iowa attorney went to college or camp or the
Army or the daycare center together, way back
when, which is the normal, rational way things
happen in this world.)

For one happy millisecond I believed the
incompetence and ignorance of my opponents'
attorneys might be *good* for me, but Morris
burst that bubble at once: "If they had a New
York guy," he explained on the phone, "somebody who knew the publishing business, he'd
know right away what the story was and what
his chances are, and we could maybe resolve
this thing. As it is, I'm on the phone to Elmira,
he's on the phone to Iowa, none of those people know what they're talking about, it's gonna
take *years* for them to gain the expertise to be
able to have a negotiation and know what the
fuck the *terms* are."

"Tell me less," I said.

But he told me more: "To begin with," he
said, "their dollar expectations are through
the roof. They see Norman Mailer, they see
Mario Puzo, they see Arthur C. Clarke, they
say, '*Each* of those guys gets millions, so a
book with all of them must be in the zillions.'
So they want a discovery proceeding on the
publisher's financial records, and you've already got three of your contributors going to
court to block any release of records pertain-
ing to *them* because they aren't part of the

suit, so that makes Iowa and Elmira doubly
suspicious, so even if they do get to see the
records, by then they won't believe them. So
they'll still want zillions."

"Tell me less, Morris," I said.

"In addition," he said, ignoring my whim-
pers, "because they don't know anything they
find it very hard to agree to anything. Initially, they were determined to hold up publication of the book until the suit was settled—"

"Oh, Jesus."

"—because they didn't want the book published without the plaintiff's name on it. Maureen Muddnyfe could breathe her last at any
minute—"

"From your lips to God's ear," I said.

"Wouldn't help," he said. "The estate could,
and certainly would, continue the suit. And if
you think it's tough to go into court and beat
the bedridden, that's *nothing* to trying to win
a judgment over the dead."

"Hell."

"Anyway, they actually went into a court-
room here in New York County—Pudney took
the stage all the way down from Elmira—and
they demanded the book not be published before resolution of the action. We finally had to
show them a couple of the contracts with contributors with the time limit on it—"

"That was Annie's idea," I said. What Annie
had done, in arranging the terms by which I
would be buying the original material for the
book, was put a time limit on our ownership

of first publication rights, and the time limit is this calendar year. It helped us get a lot of people who were otherwise reluctant to contribute, because it meant that if for some reason the book never got published, they wouldn't have to *buy* their pieces back to publish them elsewhere.

"Well, thank Annie next time you see her," Morris said, "because once Pudney understood the reversion clause—which took, I may say, considerable time—and once he had managed to communicate that understanding to the folks in Iowa, they no longer insisted on a halt in the publishing schedule."

"I should think not."

"What they want now," Morris said, "is for you and Maureen Muddnyfe to be listed as co-editors, which at least gets—"

"What?"

"—her name on the book, so she can see it before she expires. His argument—"

"Morris! I am biting the telephone!"

"—is that while this issue is still *sub judice* and not resolved, you and Mrs. Muddnyfe have equal claim to authorship and—"

"Morris Morris Morris!"

"Well, it's absurd, of course," Morris said.

"Thank you, Morris."

"But Pudney doesn't know it yet. See the problem? You know and I know, and I certainly hope the judge knows, that putting Maureen Muddnyfe's name on the book is *itself* a resolution of the suit, in her favor, but all

Pudney can see is that it will make a dying woman happy, so why are we New Yorkers all being so stony-hearted, when eventually the court will decide the issue anyway, no matter what it says on the book."

"Oh, God," I said.

"We are going to spend the next several years," Morris told me, "educating our friend Pudney in legal matters that will be of absolutely no use to him in Elmira, New York."

"And I'm paying the tuition," I said.

"You're helping," he agreed.

~~~~~~~~~~~~~~~~~~~~~~~~

Tuesday, September 27th

I have just received the most astonishing phone call. I was sitting here revising the Mayan piece for *Geo*—I am having to fudge the fact that we really don't *know* much about their interior decorating—when the phone rang and a heavy, loud, authoritative male voice barked, "Thomas J. Diskant?"

My first assumption, of course, was that this was something horrible to do with the lawsuit, and I came very close to denying my identity; but then I thought, *They'll get me anyway,* so I said, "Speaking."

"This is F. Ringwald Heffernan," the voice commanded. He sounded like a cross between a Marine drill sergeant and an oldtime factory owner.

I didn't quite catch the significance of the

name at first, still having lawsuits on the brain, so I merely said, "Yes?"

"My son told me all about that book of yours," he ordered.

"Son?"

"Dewey!"

"Dewey; Dewey *Heffernan?*"

"Certainly!"

"Wait a minute. You're . . . I'm sorry, I didn't catch the name."

"F. Ringwald Heffernan. I'm calling to tell you there won't be any more trouble from Dewey."

I stared at the phone. Who did I know who would play such a bizarre practical joke? I couldn't think of a word to say.

F. Ringwald hollered on, without my help: "He told me about that piece of trash he had that fellow draw, told me the trouble you made—"

"Oh, now—"

"—I told him, 'Goddammit, Dewey, what's the matter with you, boy? You had no business acting like that. It's that man's book, Dewey, it isn't yours, you're the *midwife*, boy. Wouldn't put up with such balderdash in *my* business, and don't you forget it.' Sat him down in the library after dinner, gave it to him straight from the shoulder."

"Oh," I said.

"Told him, 'Crawl before you fly, boy.' Told him, 'When you come to work for *me*, you'd better have all this nonsense out of your system.' Told him, 'I sent you out into the world to make your mistakes and get them over with, and they're turning out to be beauts.' Told him, 'Any more of this and I take the car keys.' Straightened him right up."

"I guess you did," I said.

"Got a pencil?"

I lunged for one. "Yes, sir!"

"Write this down. Area code two oh three. Four six five, nine nine five oh. Dewey gives you any more trouble, you phone *me*."

"Thank you," I said.

"But there won't *be* any more trouble. I straightened him right up."

"Thank you," I said.

"Nice talking with you," he demanded. "Looking forward to the book."

"Thank you," I said.

"Very fond of Christmas," he decreed, and shot the phone. At least, that's what it sounded like.

I can't think about the Mayans now, not after F. Ringwald Heffernan. Could that call possibly have been on the level? I didn't recognize the voice, and it's too *weird* to be a joke. Anyway, it's time to go turn the oven on to three-twenty-five.

Done. In lieu of the Mayans, for the next half hour until Mary gets home, I'll think about my own imperiled and changing lifestyle. I don't quite know what's happening any more, except that I seem to be spending more time downtown than uptown. This is partly caused by the continuing saga of the drifting Lance, and partly by Ginger's sudden urge toward self-improvement.

Lance first. The apartment sharing with his co-worker Bradford lasted just seventeen days. On the thirteenth of this month, two weeks ago today, he moved out, and I mean *out*. He's gotten himself transferred to some other wholly-owned CBS subsidiary, doing some other arcane sociological research, but the point is that the new job is in Washington. Our nation's capital. We had a drink before he left and he said, "There's more women down there, the male-female ratio is very very good from my point of view. But better than that, I understand they've still got some women that are interested in men. Just think; never again will I be in a discussion about Givenchy." He also said they don't have herpes down there, but that sounds like fantasy.

Anyway, now that he's living in Washington he'll be performing his daddy obligations a bit differently. Every other weekend he'll take the shuttle up to New York Friday afternoon and back down to DC Sunday evening. And guess where he'll spend Friday and Saturday nights?

Well, as he himself said (while Ginger stood thin-lipped and narrow-eyed in the background), "You're not really using the office any more, Tom, and it saves me a lot of hotel money."

As for Ginger, for reasons best known to

herself she is suddenly taking two evening courses at the New School—Japanese political history on Tuesday and Thursday, European silent film on Wednesday—which has altered our lives in other ways. Three evenings a week, Gretchen and Joshua dine with their babysitter while I meet Ginger at seven thirty-five, when her courses get out, and we eat in some Village restaurant before going uptown.

Changes make more changes. Since I'm working on 17th Street and the New School is on 12th Street, it makes no sense for me to go way uptown on those days, so I hang around here when the day's work is done. I've been helping Bryan with his English homework, and Jennifer and I have a massive Scrabble tournament under way. I usually sit down at table with them and Mary, because what else would I do while they're eating dinner? I eat lightly, but nevertheless this means I'm downing two dinners three nights a week, and I'm beginning to put those pounds back on that Vickie took off.

I wonder what the Mayans did when things got too confusing.

Thursday, September 29th

YESTERDAY Hallmark said no, and today *Cosmopolitan* said no.

The Hallmark thing was just a stab in the dark anyway, but the *Cosmo* rejection is annoying. They gave me an assignment to write about the world's most famous jewels, and I did, and now it turns out some other editor there had already assigned some other writer an article on famous jewel *thefts*, so his article and my article cover an awful lot of the same territory. I'm not being rejected because *I* did it wrong, in other words, but because *they* did it wrong.

This is a thing several magazines do; assign too many articles and overlapping articles and articles they're not really sure they want, because it doesn't cost them very much. With *Cosmo's* "no" I got a tiny check, for what is called the kill fee; this means I agree to do the article for twenty-five hundred dollars, but if for any reason they choose not to run it, even if it's because of their own error, all I get for my work is fifteen per cent. Three hundred seventy-five dollars for twenty-five hundred dollars worth of work.

Theoretically, of course, I could now sell the same piece to some other magazine, but the slicks are all so specific and unique that it's usually very hard to find a commissioned piece a second home. I suppose I could retype it, not underlining every fourth word, but it would still have the *Cosmo* girl's magpie approach, and what other magazine will want (a) a survey of world-famous jewels (b) told in the style of a rapacious ninny? I'll ask Mary when she gets home, she sometimes has good ideas on things like this.

Yesterday she had a potentially *very* good idea, in re *Happy Happy Happy*, the greeting card book. After Annie called to say that Hallmark wasn't interested and that she would now start making submissions to publishers while continuing to look for a patron among other card companies, Mary and I talked about the situation over coffee, and she suggested I take some of the completed sections, where my research and illustrations are in place, and turn them into magazine articles, maybe for somebody like *Family Circle* or *Woman's Day* or *Parade* or even *Redbook*. If we could get a few of them published that way, it would not only make the work start paying for itself but might also help to attract both a book publisher and a greeting card company sponsor. I called Annie with the suggestion this morning, and she's pondering it. Meantime, I'm going through the material, basting it into a group of potential articles.

Last night, over dinner in a Thai place called Toon's on Bleecker Street, Ginger suddenly gave me an ultimatum that I'm still wondering what to do about. "If you're going to live with *me*, Tom," she said, "*live* with me. Several people have told me how sorry they are we split up, and when I say we haven't split up they inform me, as though they think I'm the dimmest bulb in the world, that you've moved back in with Mary."

"People make mistakes," I said.

"Don't *you* make one," she said. "Come back uptown, work in your office the way you used to, stop all this ambiguity."

"Lance is—"

"*Stop* that! Lance is here *every other weekend*, that's all he's here! All his things are out of your office now, the place is just empty almost all the time, there's no *reason* for this!"

"My research material is spread all over the—"

"Pack it up!"

I said, "Ginger, there's no reason to. Everything's fine just as it is."

"Are you living with *Mary*," she wanted to know, "or are you living with *me*?"

"You, of course. I'm not *sleeping* with Mary, if that's what you want to know."

"You're not sleeping very much with me either," she informed me.

"We've both been busy," I said, because in truth our sex life has slackened somewhat since the end of summer.

"Tom," she said, "do you know what next Wednesday is?"

Was this a change of subject? It didn't feel like it, somehow. "No," I said. "What is it?"

"The fifth of October," she said sententiously, and sat there looking at me.

The fifth of October. Not her birthday, not anybody's birthday that I know. Not a holiday. Guy Fawkes is the fifth of November. I shook my head. "I don't get it."

"Our second anniversary," she said.

Anniversary? Oh, for God's sake, it was the first time we went to bed together two years ago! Like Mary remembering the date I left home!

"Our anniversary." I shook my head, not quite believing it.

She pointed a chopstick at me. "If you haven't moved *completely* back into the apartment by next Wednesday," she announced, "you needn't come back at all."

I looked at her. "Is that an ultimatum?"

"I knew there was a word for it," she said.

Thursday, October 6th

I have finished unpacking my office once again, I am back here in these familiar surroundings, and I'm still recovering from all that happened yesterday.

Yesterday. The famed October fifth, the second anniversary of the coupling of Tom and Ginger, memorialized in the form of an ultimatum from Ginger to Tom, ordering him either to bring his office home or to get out forever.

I had a week to dither over that selection, and so I did, hoping it would go away of its own accord, that Ginger would forget or change her mind or in some other fashion back away from the precipice, but yesterday morning she made it clear her attitude had not and would not change: "Don't meet me after school tonight, Tom," she said.

"Why not?"

"Because you'll be *here*," she said, "unpacking all your research materials. I'll come straight home from school and we can eat in tonight."

"Ah," I said while a cold hard hairball formed inside my ribcage. "So you still want to make an issue of that, do you?"

"Not at all," she said. "There's no issue. Either you're here or you aren't."

I could think of nothing just then to reply, though in the subway heading downtown a bit later I did engage in several impassioned interior monologues whose compelling logic, I lied to myself, would have left Ginger without an argument to her name. (Had I really had that much faith in my killer points, I could always have phoned her at her office once I got to mine—up-till-then mine—but somehow I didn't feel quite up to it.)

In the morning, I worked on query letters for greeting card articles, but my heart wasn't in it. I spent most of the time mooning out the window at the airshaft, wondering by what absurd paths I had come to this crossroads. And what further absurd paths might still stretch out ahead.

Mary and I had lunch together, and I told her at last about Ginger's ultimatum, saying, "She's jealous of you, you know."

"That is silly, isn't it?" she said, smiling a bit wistfully. "It should be the other way around."

"It isn't?"

"Oh, of course it is." Watching her spoon stir soup, she said, "Ginger's just *afraid* of losing you. I've lost you."

"Come on, Mary," I said.

She looked up at me, an inquiring expression on her face. "You really don't like being wanted, do you? A lot of men would bask in it, having two women want them, but it just makes you nervous."

"Things that make trouble make me nervous," I said.

She reached out to put her hand over mine, then apparently thought better of it and removed the hand. "I do miss you," she said. "I think it's been harder with you half-here like this. I've stopped telling you I want you back—"

"I know." I resisted the impulse to add, *And I'm grateful.*

"I didn't want to be the one to disturb the equilibrium."

"You can always count on Ginger to disturb the equilibrium."

She laughed, then said, "The mistake I made, I gave you the idea it was some kind of contest between us. If you stay away you win the contest, but if you come back I win. But it isn't like that at all, it really isn't, Tom."

Actually, it was exactly like that, an idea I'd never quite formulated for myself but which Mary had just very clearly and succinctly put into words. It *was* a contest; one of the reasons I was staying away was because I didn't want to lose. I smiled at her, shaking my head, saying, "I think we're both more mature than that."

"Do you?" She pondered that, studying her soup. "Maybe so," she said.

After lunch, bowing to the inevitable, I packed up all my papers and books into two liquor store cartons and a plastic shopping bag that said, "Have a nice day." Mary had gone out right after we ate, so there were no awkward goodbyes. The typewriter, the two cartons and the shopping bag made a cumbersome burden, but I shlepped them down to the sidewalk, found a cab, traveled uptown, shlepped everything into the building and into the elevator and into the apartment and into the office, made myself a drink, watched the television news, at last unpacked everything, and had just about finished recreating my workspace—thousands of things taped and tacked to the walls, piled on the radiator cover, stacked on the spare chair—when Ginger came in from class. She entered the office, looked around at the familiar mess with a nod and a smile of satisfaction and triumph, and said, "There. That wasn't so much trouble, was it?"

"Ginger," I said. "I have something to tell you."

She looked at me, calm and happy, and in her eyes I could see her preparing to let me

have my little face-saving statement, whatever it might be. "Yes?"

"I'm leaving you," I said.

I was astonished to hear me say that, but
nowhere near as astonished as Ginger, who
stared at me in absolute paralysis, her face
melting like Vincent Price's statues in *House
of Wax*. She didn't argue, didn't tell me I
must be kidding, didn't say a word at all. She
just stood there while I picked up the phone
and dialed. When Mary answered, I said, "Can
I come home now?"

Mary laughed; uproarious laughter, her face
turned partly away from the phone. I waited
through it, grinning sheepishly, while Ginger
burned a pure white in the corner of my eye,
and at last Mary said, "Yes, Tom, of course.
Come on home."

I hung up, put one of the liquor store cartons on the desk, and started taking things off
the wall. And at last Ginger spoke, one word
only: "Why?"

"Because," I said, "when I get down there,
Mary won't smile the way you did just now."

"That's not a reason."

"It's one of them."

She watched me for a while as I repacked
the cartons, then went away to the kitchen
and made banging and crashing noises. Ginger is not famous for taking things calmly, so
I packed as rapidly as I could, wanting if
possible to be out of there before the storm
broke.

I was on the second carton when she returned to the doorway and stood there again, watching, a drink in her hand. After a minute, she said, "I won't put up with this, you know."

I said nothing, just kept packing.

"If you go," she said, "you don't come back. I'm not Mary. I'm nobody's doormat."

"I was wrong, Ginger," I said, packing and packing. "I owe you an apology. I owe everybody an apology. I wasn't leaving Mary, after all. I thought I was, but I wasn't."

"It took you two years to find that out?"

"I'm slow," I said.

"You're a truly terrible creep," she told me.

"Probably so, probably so."

"And what happens to *me*?"

"You're a survivor," I told her. "Don't worry about yourself."

"Because *you're* certainly not going to worry about me."

"Gee, I'm not," I said, rather surprised at the discovery. I paused in my packing to face her frankly and say, "Ginger, we both knew this wasn't permanent. Remember on your birthday, when I got all weird and asked you to marry me? I've never seen anybody look so horrified in my life."

"You were drunk."

"Of course I was. Fortunately, you still had your wits about you. We've both known," I said, "that this would end some day. The only difference is, we both thought it would end when *you* were ready."

"I did know it," she agreed, nodding heavily, rather like Medea. "I knew that bitch would get you back some day."

I masking-taped the top of the second carton, dropped the roll of tape into the shopping bag, picked up both cartons. "Looks like you were right," I said, and carried the cartons away to the front door.

When I returned, she hadn't moved, was still in the doorway with arms folded and drink at the ready under her chin. She watched me pick up the typewriter and shopping bag—"Have a *nice* day," it said—and as I edged past her she narrowed her eyes to teeny tiny slits and said, "You deserve each other."

"I hope so," I said.

In the cab on the way downtown, cartons at both elbows, typewriter on lap, shopping bag somewhere around my ankles, I replayed the conversation in my mind, with emphasis on the parts that had referred to Mary, beginning with the finish, and the question of whether I deserved her. Plus Ginger's earlier comparison of herself with Mary and her use of the word "doormat."

It would be stupid, I told myself, merely to exchange one set of guilts for another. I have behaved badly toward Mary, and toward a whole lot of other people—Gretchen comes to mind—but Mary seems willing to forgo the pleasures of resentment and moral superiority for the less certain but more complex pleasures of the *status quo ante*. If I am incapable of taking her at face value, if I go downtown prepared only to be hangdog and ashamed of myself, what's the point in going? What have I accomplished? The object of all this thrashing around is to make it possible to *stop* thrashing around.

On the other hand, to arrive on 17th Street whistling and carefree, without any acknowledgment of what I've put Mary through for twenty months, would be exactly treating her, in Ginger's word, as a doormat. And in fact she wouldn't put up with that. I know Mary; I know her limits. What Ginger misreads as passivity I understand to be self-knowledge and strength. "Uhh, cabby," I said, through the bullet holes in the Lucite, "stop at a florist, will you?" The dumb-cluck, little-boy errant husband always comes home with flowers.

Mary laughed when she saw them; they were in my teeth. The long cone of florist's paper dangled down my front like some surrealist necktie while I bit down hard on the bunched paper at the cone's base, tasting staple, in the meantime carrying everything else. "Let me help you with that," she said, took the flowers, turned them right side up, and closed the door after me as I staggered in.

Reeling a bit, I lunged my way through the apartment and left my office in the office. Mary meanwhile had gone to the kitchen to put the flowers in water in a vase, so I followed her in there and said, "Mary, I'm sorry."

She shook her head. "That isn't important, Tom," she said. "Thank you for saying it, but that isn't what matters. People are sorry about things all the time, that's as easy as breathing. Right now, I can hear myself, I sound stuffy and bloodless and I wish I wasn't like that, so I'm sorry about it, but it doesn't help, I'm still that way."

"No, you're not. My God, just because you aren't screaming all the time—"

"But I am." She glanced at me, then stepped back to consider the flower arrangement in the vase. "You just can't hear me, that's all," she said.

I had to put my arms around her then, and stop talking, and I'm not sure which of us was trembling more. I kissed her mouth and her cheeks, tasting salt, and finally I said, "I *am* sorry."

"No," she said. "That's the wrong word."

Arms still around her, I leaned back to see her expression. "It is?"

She smiled at me, and at last I understood it's all right for Mary to indulge me, because when she does it there's no contempt in it. "Do you know why I believed you'd come back?" she asked me.

"No, I don't."

"Because in all of your explanations and all of your reasons and all of your statements of belief, there was one word you never used when you talked about you and Ginger."

"I have trouble with that word," I said.

She smiled again. "You use it sometimes."

This was to be one of the times. "I love you," I said.

~~~~~~~~~~~~~~~

Friday, October 7th

IS it as though I've never been away?

Wednesday night, I wasn't sure if Mary and I would or should go to bed together, so I dithered about it until she reached up to grab my jaw and shake my head, saying, "Tom, *I* haven't had a friend on the side for the last nineteen months. That's a *long* time. And don't say you're sorry."

"I didn't plan to say a word," I assured her, though some time later I did say, "Thank you," which made her laugh again. And yesterday morning she was the one who said, "Thank you," adding, "We'll have to do that at least three times a day for a good long while to get caught up."

"I'll give it my full attention," I said. "But *you* aren't going to be ogled and fondled and propositioned by all those guys out there in the world any more."

"Of course not. When they look at me, they'll see you in my eyes."

"You bet they will."

Which was the only moment she showed any uncertainty at all. About to get out of bed, she paused to look back over her shoulder, frowning slightly. "Tom," she said, "you *are* home to stay, aren't you?"

"You bet I am."

"Why?"

"Because you wouldn't put up with it twice," I said. "And I do love you, Mary, and I don't want to lose you."

She smiled, saying, "I wasn't sure you'd realize that."

"I'm beginning to catch on. You probably even know what you'd do if it happened again."

"I'd leave New York," she said.

I nodded, knowing I'd known that, and feeling scared, because I just might have been dumb enough not to know it. To avoid looking in the abyss, I said, "Do you know where you'd go?"

And that made her laugh, too. "Helena's been writing me," she said.

"Helena?"

"Lance's old girlfriend, the one who went to—"

"Santa Fe!" I said, remembering. "The one who forced Lance back into Ginger's apartment!" Which started the chain of events, really.

"That's right. She's been writing me for months, saying I should take the children out of school and move to Santa Fe."

"What a bitch!"

"She says I could take wonderful pictures there."

"All those sunsets," I said. "Cactus. Pick-up trucks. Golly."

"She says it's wonderful in Santa Fe. She says the men there aren't insecure," she added, openly laughing at me.

"Oh, sure they are," I said, but I hunkered down under the covers for a few extra minutes.

If the kids were surprised to see me that early in the morning, they were too hip to show it. (On the other hand, if they *weren't* surprised to see me, they're too hip to think about.) We sat around the kitchen table together, me with my coffee and Mary with a plain yogurt and the kids with Cap'n Crunch and peanut butter and jelly on English muffin and orange juice and a sliced-up banana and coffee with lots of milk (Bryan) and Earl Grey tea (Jennifer). We talked about nothing in particular, and when the kids left for school Jennifer said, "See you tonight," almost but not quite making it a question. "See you tonight," I told her.

In the grandness and folly of my round-trip renunciation on Wednesday, I'd forgotten that all work and no play makes Tom a naked

man. I'd brought my office home, but all my
clothing was still up at Ginger's place. Therefore, early yesterday afternoon I called her
apartment, got my own voice telling me to
call where I was calling from (which meant
the coast was clear), and then cabbed uptown, let myself in with my keys, and went
into the bedroom to see if Ginger had taken
the scissors to all my shirts, in traditional
scorned-woman style.

No. Nothing of mine in either the bedroom
or bathroom had been touched, and I was
surprised and somewhat touched to realize
Ginger expected me back. She thought we
were still dancing the mating dance, that we
were still just doing things to keep our interest up, and so she wouldn't do anything irre-
vocable. Once she understood that she was
dancing alone, that the music had stopped,
then she would be *really* mad.

I packed. I left my keys on the kitchen table, and went away. I would have done something about my voice on the answering machine, but what was there to do? "This is Tom
Diskant, I'm not here right now, call me at
. . ." and so on. Well, exactly. Everything in
the world was topsy-turvy, and my answering
machine message was still accurate.

~~~~~~~~~~~~~~~~~~~~~

Tuesday, October 11th

THE CHRISTMAS BOOK! At last.

I have held a copy in my hands. It is beside me on the desk as I type, and it is *beautiful*. All the hassles, all the trouble, the three editors, everything, it was all worth it. The book is big and gorgeous and thoughtful and rich and magnificent. My introduction isn't as pompous as I'd feared, and the cheap color reproduction process looks great.

Dewey called this morning, about eleven-thirty, to say the books were in. This is a test run, about twenty-five copies or so to make sure everything's working well (and in fact there are a couple of pages with color problems and a few last-minute corrections and improvements), and then on Thursday they'll actually start the print run. The test copies were driven to the Craig offices from the printer in Pennsylvania this morning, and when they arrived Dewey phoned and offered to messenger a copy down to me.

It was a changed Dewey. This is the first I've spoken with him since that astounding phone call from his putative father, and I guess old F. Ringwald Heffernan must have been on the level after all, because this was a subdued and friendly and accommodating Dewey, obviously doing his best to make amends. "It's a really terrific book, Tom," he said, and actually added, "I think you were right that the other thing didn't really fit in."

"Thank you, Dewey," I said, prepared to be magnanimous.

We talked a bit more, and then he said, "Are you working on anything in particular at the moment, Tom?"

I had ordered Annie not to submit *Happy Happy Happy* to Craig. "Oh, this and that," I said.

"The reason I ask, I presented a book idea to Mr. Wilson, and he said okay, and now I'm supposed to find a writer."

Have bygones ever more swiftly become bygones? "Well, I'm not actually *tied up* with other work, Dewey," I said. "What is this book?"

"The history of video games."

"The history of video games?" It hadn't occurred to me that video games had been around long enough to *have* a history.

But apparently so. "Sure," he said. "From

the earliest chess computers, and forerunners like pinball and slot machines. And don't forget Tommy!"

"Tommy?"

"*Tommy, the Pinball Wizard*, the rock opera by The Who. *There's* a historic moment in pop culture!"

"Ah," I said. The old Dewey had not been entirely repressed after all.

"I'm afraid I can't offer you much more than you got on *The Christmas Book*," he said. "Your share, I mean."

My mouth dry, I said, "But a *little* more, surely?" as though we were all just calmly bandying words about.

"Well, I guess everybody has to get a little more every time," he said, and laughed self-consciously. "I'm starting to learn this business."

I was dying to ask him about his father, but I was afraid it would embarrass him; and maybe he didn't know about that call. I said, "I'll have Annie phone you, work out the details."

"Annie?"

"My agent," I said. "Have you learned that much about the business?"

"Oh, yes," he said. "I know about agents. They're always trying to pull something."

"Not my Annie," I assured him. "She's very motherly and nice. You'll like her."

"Okay," he said doubtfully. Then he promised again to messenger the book, and we hung up, and he did messenger the book, and here it is!

And I'm about to get big bucks for another book!

And I'm back with Mary, back in the bosom of my family and loving it!

Life is okay after all.

~~~~~~~~~~~~

Friday, October 14th

AT eight a.m. yesterday morning, the print-
ers and warehousemen and other skilled crafts-
men at the Heritage Consolidated Press in
Potted Pine, Pennsylvania, went out on strike.
Clerical workers and other employees left at
noon, in sympathy. The union contract ex-
pired last June thirtieth, and the employees
have been working without a contract while
negotiations have continued. The employees
decided to go out at this precise moment because Heritage Consolidated was about to start
on its single largest order of the year: *The
Christmas Book*.

As usual, a union goes on strike to pressure
not the employer but some third party—in
this case, Craig, Harry & Bourke—in hopes
the third party will apply direct pressure on
the employer to settle the dispute to the union's

satisfaction. According to Robert Wilson, head honcho at Craig, who phoned me personally this morning to give me the news—this is perhaps the third time I've spoken with him in my life—this time the union's strategy is unlikely to work. Not only does Craig have very little pressure it can bring to bear on Heritage Consolidated, but Heritage Consolidated has apparently been prepared to shut this plant down for some time—they have others, mostly in the south—and are willing to treat an extended strike as a de facto closing, which would be a lot cheaper than if the deed were done the proper way, with severance pay and all the rest of it.

Unless the strike is settled by the end of *next week,* there will be no copies of *The Christmas Book* at Christmas.

Because of Annie's reversion clause, if there is no *Christmas Book* this year, there is no *Christmas Book.*

There is no *Christmas Book.*

Friday, November 25th

I am still recuperating from yesterday, Thanksgiving Day. A true harvest festival, the closest thing in Puritan America to real hedonism, the one day a year when gluttony is not only acceptable but required. (Another of the seven deadly sins memorialized.)

While it is true that the first Thanksgiving Day was celebrated as a sit-down harvest gala among the early Pilgrims and some tame neighborhood Indians, the feast did not become a national holiday until 1863, when Abraham Lincoln issued a proclamation on the subject. Proclamations kept the holiday alive year by year until 1941, when Congress made it a permanent addition to the American calendar.

Lincoln's proclamation—Thanksgiving, not emancipation—was done at the urging of one

Sarah Josepha Hale, then editor of *Godey's Lady's Book*, who was also the author of "Mary Had a Little Lamb," among other works, and who, an ardent feminist, persuaded Vassar Female College, founded in 1861, to delete the word "Female" from its name in 1867. If she'd stopped to think how many American women down through the decades would be struggling to cook (without drying them out) twenty-two pound turkeys on the fourth Thursday of every November, she might well have told Lincoln to forget it.

It's been six weeks since I added anything to this history; not since labor and management got together out there in Pennsylvania to kill my baby. I understand the strike is still going on, is likely to last a lot longer, and has begun to spread to some of the company's southern plants as well. It looks as though both sides are going to suffer a lot. Good.

There is no *Christmas Book*, but good things did come of it. The money, for instance; the lack of a book wasn't my fault, nor the contributors' fault, so we all got to keep our payments. And then there's *Highest Previous Score*, which is our working title for the history of video games. Since my track record now includes the money I was paid for *The Christmas Book*, Annie got me a *much* higher advance for *Highest Previous Score* than would have happened last year. (Beat my highest previous score, in fact.) Also, Dewey continues to combine contriteness for past misdeeds with a wonderful galumphing enthusiasm for this new book, so it may even get good support from the company when it comes out next September. (It'll be next year's Craig, Harry & Bourke Christmas book, of course.)

And video games are really interesting when you get to know about them, in a way. Sort of. Well, bearable, anyway. (There's something I wouldn't tell anybody but Mary, which is the truth: Video games are even more boring to read about and write about than to play. But what I am is a professional, and what *Highest Previous Score* is is what they'll pay me to write. Listen, it could be Erik Estrada's autobiography.)

But what made me think about *The Christmas Book* again is something that came in the mail today, from Pompano Beach, Florida: a birth announcement. "Mr. and Mrs. Harold J. Goldbaum are pleased to announce the birth of their daughter, Tiffany Rachel Goldbaum," et cetera. At first I couldn't figure out why Mr. and Mrs. Harold J. Goldbaum, of whom I have never before heard, wanted to share this glad news with me, but then all at once the penny dropped and I said out loud, "Vickie!"

Has to be. I counted backward, and from what she told me she should be almost due now, so she dropped the kid a couple weeks early, which would be very much in character, she being sort of jumpy and neurotic and impatient. I cannot begin to picture Harold, but whoever he is he clearly didn't stand a chance.

So; the publishing world's loss is Florida's gain. I hope she'll be— Well, not happy, let's stay within the range of the possible. I hope she'll be reasonably content part of the time.

Speaking of happiness, Hubert Van Driin of Federalist Press has agreed to take *Happy Happy Happy*, for a shitty amount of money. It's on the back burner right now, because of *Highest Previous Score*, but if the deal with Coca-Cola works out this book too might become a winner. Indirectly, this is also a result of *The Christmas Book*.

It all began with the Andy Warhol contribution, the Coca-Cola tray with Santa Claus on it. I cut out that middleman by dealing directly with a Coca-Cola PR lady in Atlanta. Naturally, she's one of the people I informed when the book was murdered, and just last week she phoned to say she was in town for a few days on Coca-Cola business, and could we talk.

So we talked. Her name is Lynn Mulligan, she's tall and quite attractive, early thirties, and in truth she was in New York because she'd talked the company into relocating her to their advertising liaison office in New York. Seems her marriage recently came to an end, so she wants to pick up the kids and move out of Atlanta. She'll make the move after Christmas, so what she initially wanted to talk about was apartments and schools and all the rest of it.

But then the subject of *Happy Happy Happy* came up, and when I described our failure to get Hallmark to sponsor and subsidize the project, she suddenly said, "We might."

"You might what?"

"Be interested in the book. Will it be published by next fall?"

"It could be," I said.

"If Coca-Cola could get some placement in the book," she said, "maybe something on the jacket and title page—"

"Lovely," I said. "But why?"

"Well, we might take a printing," she said, "make it the corporate Christmas present next year. Say twenty, twenty-five thousand copies."

Hubert Van Driin has been known to do hardcover printings of specialized nostalgia books of twenty-five *hundred* copies. If I go into his office with one customer's order for twenty-five thousand, his gaiters will absolutely *snap*. His bow tie will spin like an airplane propeller. He'll have to go home and change his trousers.

Lynn is back in Atlanta now, laying the groundwork for the idea, and I won't know until after the first of the year, but I am very hopeful. On the other hand, I am for the moment leaving *Happy* on the back burner, to concentrate on *Highest Previous Score;* I have seen great expectations sag before.

Whether this Coca-Cola deal works out or

not, my having met Lynn at least proved one thing to me; I'm home for good. If I were on the alert for another Ginger, by golly, here she is. And she made it clear she wouldn't hate it if I made overtures.

But I did not, and I won't. I remember now why Mary and I got together in the first place, and it was because we belonged together. I'd allowed myself to forget that over the years. With Mary the only steadfastness in this constantly shifting and ridiculous life, it became easier and easier not to notice her.

Or, that is, not to notice any but the bad parts, the little annoyances and irritations that every one of us distributes like a squid's surrounding cloud of ink. Mary's dogged determination to become a first-class photographer, for instance, when she just simply was not graced with that gift. She doesn't *do* anything about being a first-class photographer, just gets up every morning as the same old bush-league picture-taker and takes some more bush-league pictures, in the calm hope (not expectation, merely hope) that some magic transformation would have taken place in her eye and mind since yesterday.

In fact, her very calm, her bulldog staying power that looks so suspiciously like passivity but somehow is not, can become annoying. The smell of chemicals in the bathroom, there's another. The fact that she usually knows more about me than I do. All of that ink gradually filled the foreground, obscuring the large and more important truths. And so, self-bewitched, forgetting I already had the Blue Rose, out I went in quest of it. That's not a mistake I'll make twice. (Apart from anything else, Jennifer and Bryan would *hate* Santa Fe.)

Saturday, December 24th

I have just been assembling a bicycle. Do I
look like somebody who ought to be assembling a bicycle? Particularly with instructions
translated from the Korean into some distant
relative of English: "And the other hexagonal
nut, interchange is made from the chrome bar
through."

Well, I'm through, and I've been to the bar.
The Christmas tree has been trimmed, the
presents assembled and assembled (if you see
what I mean), Mary and I have drunk champagne and have made long lingering love on
the living room sofa, and now she has gone to
bed and I have roamed the house, restless, at
last coming into the office to stand a while
and hold *The Christmas Book* in my hand. One
of the very few copies. What a nice book it is.

One unpleasant surprise was that the death

of the book was not the death of the lawsuit. That, Morris assures me, will continue into the indefinite future. The Muddnyfes want my advance, plus punitive damages. Morris says it's probably four or five years before I'll have to think about the suit again, but I bet the memory of it will cross my mind from time to time in the days to come.

Ginger's boy Joshua is still best pals with Bryan, and was here for a while this afternoon, so now I have an update on the Patchett family. Gretchen has won some sort of interborough grade school art contest, the prizes including an easel and various art materials, and is apparently in seventh heaven. Lance, who is in New York for the holidays, has announced he's moving to Los Angeles after the first of the year, so I guess the women in Washington didn't pan out after all. And Ginger is now palling around with a United Nations diplomat from Nigeria; the fellow's wife and kids are in Lagos, and therefore less likely to be a distraction.

One of the necessary components in the recipe of life appears to be regret. We regret those things we cannot fix. Bit by bit I am fixing the harm I did to Mary and Jennifer and Bryan. I don't believe I left anything to fix with either Ginger or Vickie, but one thing I do continue to regret: I will never be able to make it up to Gretchen.

If I had slipped one of her drawings into *The Christmas Book*, I could have wangled a second copy of the test run from the repentant Dewey, and now Gretchen could have that; an unpublished book with her drawing and her name in it. Because what does unpublication mean to a kid? She'd get a charge out of the book, no matter what.

Well, so do I, really. From time to time I pick it up and browse in it, which is exactly what you're supposed to do with a Christmas book anyway. And the other day I looked again, for the first time in months, at my introduction, and all of a sudden I realized what, all unconsciously, I had been doing. (Most of the things I do are unconscious, I'm afraid.)

INTRODUCTION

There is a tidal pull in great simple ideas, nowhere more evident than in the great simple idea of Christmas. It begins as a mere birthday, in deceptively plain circumstances, but at once the event resonates, becomes more and larger than itself, becomes in fact something other than itself. Because Christmas is not after all the birthday of God; that is surely Easter, when Christ does what only a God can do of His own volition: He rises from the dead. Christmas is something simpler than that, clearer, more understandable and less disputable: Christmas is the birth of the family.

It is this that gives Christmas its partic-

*ular role in our lives, and that makes it
at the same time both so banal and so compelling, why we sometimes wish to avoid
it but never can. Other public days remember love, or labor, or freedom, or some moment of history, but the basic Christmas
image is that mundane trinity: the father, the mother, and the Child whose existence brings the family into being.*

  *Christmas reminds us we are not alone.
We are not unrelated atoms, jouncing and
ricocheting amid aliens, but are a part of
something, which holds and sustains us.
As we struggle with shopping lists and in-
vitations, compounded by December's bad
weather, it is good to be reminded that there
are people in our lives who are worth this
aggravation, and people to whom we are
worth the same. Christmas shows us the
ties that bind us together, threads of love
and caring, woven in the simplest and
strongest way within the family.*

A year ago I presented Jack Rosenfarb with
a book project, and I thought I was doing it so
I could stay away from my family; get the
money to make continued absence possible,
break Mary's determination to wait. And look
at the project I came up with. Here in the
book we have Puzo and Galbraith and Beattie
and King and McDowall and I don't know
who all, hitting the same subject time after
time; the family, and its interconnection. With-

out noticing, I spent half a year trying to put a fire out by pouring kerosene on it.

I wish I had some vision other than hindsight, but I guess that will have to do. I am home, I appear to be happy, and all my problems are small ones: a million dollar lawsuit, a tenuous handhold on the lower rung of an imbecile industry, and the growing suspicion that I am that dullest of all creatures, a family man.

Oh, well, what the hell. Merry Christmas, everybody.

BESTSELLING BOOKS FROM TOR

MORE BESTSELLERS FROM TOR

RICHARD HOYT

"Richard Hoyt is an expert writer."
—*The New York Times*